A Beth-Hill Novel:
Full Moon

By Jennifer St. Clair

Writers Exchange E-Publishing

http://www.writers-exchange.com

A Beth-Hill Novel: Full Moon
Copyright 2008, 2015, 2023 Jennifer St. Clair
Writers Exchange E-Publishing
PO Box 372
ATHERTON QLD 4883

Cover Art by: Jatin and Sandy Cummins

Published by Writers Exchange E-Publishing
http://www.writers-exchange.com

Chapter 1

In the cramped space of the dog crate, human fingers slipped through the bars and lifted the latch. Perhaps at some point they would put a lock on their cages and he would not be able to escape. They would kill him when his time was up, his body disposed of like so much waste.

Perhaps it would be better that way. Edward pushed that thought away as soon as it appeared. If he let them win--if he just *gave up,* then what would he have lived for all of these years? He'd survived his curse for over a century; to give up now seemed every bit a terrible defeat.

He stood, eyeing the dogs around him, but they remained silent, watching and wary, as they had since he'd arrived. For a moment, he thought about freeing them all, just so the keepers of the keys wouldn't search for only one dog. But the scars that crisscrossed his body--from encounters with wild dogs near his sanctuary--reminded him of gnashing teeth and growling fury, so he left them there and retreated into the kitchen.

He stole a bottle of water to wash away the taste of the food they had fed him, and found someone's forgotten lunch in the fridge when he opened the door. Just the thought of *real* food made him weak; he had to sit down at the tiny table to open the bag and examine the contents. To a stomach used to the odd bird or rabbit, a chicken sandwich seemed almost too good to be true, especially since a chicken had landed him here in the first place.

A further search of the kitchen turned up a forgotten coat--not as thick as he would have wished to wear against the weather outside, but good enough--and someone's dirty exercise clothes that would help protect him from the snow. The shoes didn't fit, but a pair of rubber boots they wore to spray out the kennels did, and those would do as well as anything.

He found forty dollars in a desk drawer, and took that too, knowing that he could stop at a store, perhaps, on the way home, and buy food this time--*human* food--instead of whatever half-starved game he could catch. This winter had been brutal. And it wasn't over yet.

But when he stepped up to the glass doors and stared out at the driving snow, he wondered if he had enough strength to get back home. He knew which way his house stood--far to the east--but the trek through the snow would be perilous, indeed. He touched the glass with one hand and shivered at the cold.

Something whined behind him. Edward tensed, half-expecting teeth to tear into his flesh, but nothing happened, save for the appearance of a dark shadow in the window. When he turned, the black and white dog that had somehow followed him shied away.

"You don't want to come with me," Edward said, unable to raise his voice above a whisper. When was the last time he had actually *spoken* to someone? Did a dog *count?*

The dog whined again, took a small step forward, then froze, as if waiting for him to reprimand her. But she had done nothing wrong.

"I can't feed myself," Edward whispered, and turned back towards the door again. "How would I be able to feed *you?*" He closed his eyes against the wind and pushed open the door, and something brushed past him as he stepped into searing cold and let the door swing shut behind him.

Hot tears thawed his skin, then froze on his face as the wind brought a scattering of snow across the desolation. The tears blurred the streetlights around him, making them a strange smear of white in a symphony of darkness.

The dog stopped a few feet away, wagging her tail, obviously waiting for him to make the first move.

After a moment, knowing he had to move or freeze to death, he shuffled forward, towards home. He had no true idea how long it would take to reach his refuge, but he thought he might make it by dawn.

If the weather didn't kill him first.

With the lingering memory of the warmth of the animal shelter in his mind, Edward dug his hands into the pockets of his stolen jacket and set his sights on home.

The dog followed. He did not have the heart to send her away.

Chapter 2

"Healers are usually called *before* the patient dies," Sennet said, and tried to keep the irritation out of her voice. "Why am I here?"

"You are an impartial party to the succession," Ceidrin said, and made a face. "Believe me, this was *not* my decision, or my suggestion. I would have left you in peace."

The Queen of this particular kingdom in Faerie had died mere weeks before from an illness that sounded suspicious even to Sennet's ears. She'd left no direct heirs and a messy succession--according to Ceidrin, her cousin and her cousin's son were closest to the throne--and one of them had probably hastened her demise. But Sennet had not come to unmask a murderer. Instead, they had asked her to come to watch the proceedings. As if her presence alone would make it well and good.

"I shouldn't be here," she said again. "This isn't--"

Ceidrin held up his hand to forestall her protests. "Please. All you have to do is be present. You don't have to speak, you don't have to react to any of the proceedings--although if Meinren is crowned king, I may have to protest."

"Is his the hand that administered the poison?" Sennet asked, only half-joking.

Ceidrin's face paled. "I would not say that again," he said, and hurried her through the corridor, past a vast array of paintings and mosaics made with precious stones. He entered a small empty room--there were more empty rooms than full ones in the castle, it seemed--and muttered a spell to check for eavesdroppers. "I've not been back here for a century, at least. I've heard stories about what happened, of course; whispered ones only. No one will come right out and say it, but she did not deserve this death."

"You weren't here when it happened, then," Sennet said, and wondered if he had asked her to come to prevent any *other* deaths.

"No. I was--" He shrugged. "Elsewhere. And I would *prefer* to be elsewhere now. However, as a cousin to the Queen, I am summoned just like everyone else."

"And where do *you* stand in line for the throne?" Sennet asked.

Ceidrin's mouth twisted. "It depends. Since our Queen left no direct heirs, this will be an interesting succession."

"Hmm." Sennet wandered over to where another painting hung on the wall; this one darkened with age. "Any chance--"

"No." Ceidrin's tone of voice left no room for speculation. "I would not want it, regardless. Meinren and Oriellen technically have dibs, as it were. There are two others--Elinor and Lucien--who have a better chance than me, and both of them have...issues of their own. The rest of us can only seethe." He joined her at the painting, and pointed to a young girl. "That was our Queen, a long, long time ago. Isabel."

"And the rest?" Sennet asked. There were six people in the painting, two adults, both crowned, so obviously the king and queen of long ago, and four children, one of them still a toddler. Three girls and one boy.

"Those were her parents," Ceidrin said, and pointed them out. "Aelfyn and Citrinia. The boy was her brother, who died in a hunting accident when he was young. His name was Jeremin. This--" he pointed to the baby, "Oriellen. Hence the reason why Oriellen and Meinren are the front contenders for the throne."

"And the third girl?" Sennet asked when he didn't continue.

"Her name was Nidrea," Ceidrin said shortly. "She--was Isabel's elder sister. If she had stayed, then perhaps none of this would have happened."

Nidrea had darker hair than the others, or perhaps she stood in shadow, because it was difficult to see her face. She wore a dark gown as well, and held a sword, point down, between her hands, a stiff and awkward pose. The others' props were no less intriguing: a scepter; what looked like an ornate globe; and a silver bow.

Sennet pointed to the sword. "That looks familiar."

Ceidrin snorted. "Impossible. That sword vanished with Nidrea and hasn't been seen since."

"Vanished?"

In four quick steps, Ceidrin strode to the door, opened it, and glanced out. When he was satisfied that they were well and truly alone, he closed the door, locked it, and cast a ward upon the room.

"Nidrea ran away with her human lover," he said. "That--that wasn't *done* two hundred years ago. Especially if the elf in question is the heir to the throne."

Coming from an elf who *had* a human lover, his tone of disapproval was a bit surprising. But then again, Nidrea had abandoned her post, for want of a better word.

"Is she dead?"

"If she isn't, she will be if *they* find out she's alive," Ceidrin said. "I wouldn't mention her name outside of this room." He grinned. "Now, if

Nidrea had children with her human, those *children* would have a larger claim to the throne, half-human or no. Now *that* would be an interesting succession. As it is, I think I'll be leaving again very soon."

Sennet touched the sword in the painting, half-expecting to feel something other than dirt and grime and long-dried paint under her fingers. "You told me that they requested my presence here," she said softly, not looking at him. "Was that true? Or am I here for *your* protection?"

Ceidrin stopped with his hand on the doorknob, his shoulders tense, his head lowered. "You are here...you are here because you are the only person I can trust to not stab me in the back while *I* am here."

He stated this so simply that Sennet turned to stare at him in shock. "You're serious?"

"I won't be eating while I'm here, for that matter," Ceidrin said. "Or drinking. If I--" He clenched one hand into a fist and slammed it against the door. "If I had known this would happen--"

"Don't blame yourself," Sennet said. "I'm fairly certain I can detect poison, so you needn't starve." She'd known Ceidrin long enough to realize how hard it would be for him to refrain from sampling some of the inevitable feast. It was no accident that his lover was a chef.

"You'll stay, then?" he asked, and raised his head.

"I'll stay." Sennet smiled. "Gene would kill me if I didn't." She'd met them both when a much younger Gene had almost cut off three of his fingers.

Ceidrin nodded. "He might try," he said, and tried to smile. "Thank you. Shall we go?"

"They don't know I'm here with you?" Sennet asked.

"No, they don't," Ceidrin replied, a faraway look in his eyes. "And that might be best, really. Would anyone recognize you?"

"They shouldn't," Sennet said. "I've never actually been here before."

"And yet you recognized the sword?" Ceidrin frowned. "Strange."

"I've seen it before, somewhere," Sennet said, but her memory would not supply the place. "If I remember--"

"If you remember, don't tell anyone but me," Ceidrin said, his voice intense. "Please."

"Of course," Sennet replied. "You're stalling."

This time, at least, he was able to smile. "Of course I am."

"They'll come searching for you if you don't go to them," Sennet said, and held out her hand. "Let's go."

Ceidrin hesitated, and then tucked her hand under his arm, as if he was about to promenade her into a formal gathering, which, she supposed, was more the case than not.

"Meinren is the one I'm worried about," he muttered, and opened the door. "Be wary."

"Even your cousins know the penalty for harming a Healer in the course of duty," Sennet said mildly. "Surely they wouldn't be so stupid."

"I would hope not," Ceidrin said, and pasted a very fake smile on his face. "But since they don't know you're a Healer--"

"If I have to save your life, they'll know fairly quickly," Sennet said, and let him lead her down the hall. They passed more paintings, and then, as the drift of voices echoed off the walls, a painting of Nidrea herself, seated in an ornate chair, the sword lying across her legs. She wore a simple silver crown in her honey-colored hair, but even as a painting, her grey eyes seemed troubled.

"Sennet--" Ceidrin sighed when she stopped in front of the painting. "Nidrea is a myth. She won't magically appear to save us all."

"But perhaps the succession could be postponed for a bit just in case she's still alive," Sennet said softly, and wondered if she would return if she was.

"You suggest that to the gathering, then, and see how it is received," Ceidrin grumbled, then stiffened when an elf appeared at the other end of the corridor.

"Meinren?" Sennet whispered under her breath.

"None other," Ceidrin muttered, then smiled broadly. "You aren't waiting for me, I hope?"

"Of course we are," the elf snapped. His eyes narrowed when he saw Sennet. "Who is this?"

"An uninterested party," Sennet replied before Ceidrin could speak. "Here by invitation."

"Whose invitation?" the elf asked.

"Mine," Ceidrin said, and his voice matched the elf's in tone. "And if I have to claim bloodright for her presence, I will."

The elf sniffed, glared at Ceidrin, then turned on his heel to vanish amid the voices again.

"Oh, this should be interesting," Sennet said as they approached the doors.

Ceidrin snorted. "I think I would prefer my own cooking," he said, and led her through the swinging doors.

Chapter 3

Elinor had stolen the car, but the blinding snow had forced her to use a spell to make it out of the city. Without the spell--for traction, of course--she would have been at the bottom of the river by now, despite the ice.

And perhaps, in hindsight, that would have been better. Her Aunt's hunters could have abandoned the search, and she would have been free.

Dead, but free.

She drove without spells now, because spells were worse than a paper trail to the ones who hunted her, but the roads were no better far from the city. In fact, they seemed to be a bit worse.

She thought she missed the streetlights the most; with them, at least, was the thin veneer of civilization, unlike the dark woods and empty fields that lay on either side of her now.

The countryside seemed both desolate and beautiful; despite the driving snow.

There was no map unfolding in her head; she had no true destination other than *away*. Far, far away. Because if they caught her, if Oriellen's hunters found her before she could find a place to shelter from the dawn, then she would be better off to run the car into a tree, or a telephone pole, or turn around and drive off the edge of that bridge.

Death would be a blessing if they caught her.

She refused to think of what would happen if she managed to get away. The crown wasn't even *hers*--

When the deer appeared in her headlights--a flash of tawny fur and wide brown eyes--she wrenched the steering wheel to the left, towards the field, not wanting another death to add to her list, even if it *was* only a deer.

For a moment, as she wrestled for control against the ice, she wondered if she should just allow the crash to happen. She'd freeze to death before they found her--surely she would--and then--

In the light of her headlights, silhouetted against the driving snow, standing on the side of the road with one hand up to shade his eyes and the other held close against his body, was a man.

Elinor screamed. His appearance was so...so *sudden,* so unexpected, that she released the steering wheel and threw up her hands, automatically sketching a warding sign before she remembered that she was *on the run*--and any magic would direct her Aunt's hunters to her trail before she could lose them again.

She heard and *felt* a thump as the car careened sideways--surely too soft to be the man--and then it slid to a stop, the headlights illuminating the falling snow and nothing more.

And for a moment, she sat there, gasping for air, feeling the panic of the last few hours beating down every last inch of both courage and strength.

She'd spent her winters in Faerie since she was young. Her father had lived in the human world, her mother had never left her family home. But this time, when Elinor returned, she found the house destroyed, her mother burned, and the hunters waiting for her. All because of a stupid crown.

She knew what they were doing. She knew what would happen if she didn't show up at the gathering. But it didn't matter anymore, did it? Her mother was dead.

And no one else needed to die tonight. Even before she realized she had moved, Elinor opened the car door and let the icy snow sweep the memories back where they belonged.

The cold numbed everything; from skin to fury, and the snow's soft hiss soothed her mind. She could almost believe that she was safe here, in the middle of a country road with no one around; the sound of the snowfall even masking the noise of the car's engine.

When she stepped away from the car, she saw no sign of the man. She couldn't even tell where the road ended and the field began; the snow glowed in the darkness, even though heavy clouds covered the full moon.

She thought--in passing--to use a spell to find him, but that would damn her for certain, and she had much less of a chance to wreck the car now than she had before.

And then, as she slowly made her way around the side of the car, she saw his leg, and then his body--both thankfully attached to each other--and the path of his trajectory across the asphalt, already half-covered with snow. A dog stood guard over him, a furry black and white creature who growled as she approached.

"Hush," she told it. "Hush and let me help him."

Unmindful of the cold, Elinor knelt beside him, struggling to hold back any sort of healing magic until she could take him to a well-warded place. His eyes were closed, his face pale even under a coating of snow. He wore clothes too thin for travel through a blizzard; a thin coat, rubber boots. She almost expected him to vanish when she touched his hand, or show himself to be a hunter--or worse.

The dog whined.

"He'll be fine," Elinor said, and hoped that were true. "Sir? Can you hear me?" She gently shook his shoulder, praying for a response.

But he just lay there with his eyes closed and his hair frozen to his face, his lips blue, his chest barely moving, his fingers darkened by frostbite.

And she couldn't just sit there forever and stare at him, since this was her fault.

She glanced both up and down the road, but she'd passed no cars and saw no sign of approaching vehicles. With as much care as she could manage, since he was a bit taller than her--but thin under the fragile bulk of the clothing; *too* thin--she flung one of his arms around her shoulders and dragged him to the car. The dog followed, hopping into the backseat as soon as she opened the door.

Oh well, she thought. *It's not my car anyway.*

When she lowered the man onto the backseat, he moaned, his arm twitching across her shoulders. But his eyes were still closed when she eased away from him. She covered him with a blanket she found in the trunk, then hurried around to the driver's side door as the dog watched, its eyes bright and interested.

It would not do for the hunters to find her with an innocent in this. They would not hesitate to kill him--or worse. And if Oriellen found him--she shivered.

Elinor slid behind the wheel again, and put the car into drive. With an unconscious passenger, she knew she couldn't drive as fast as she had been before--if she crashed, it would be akin to killing him herself.

"He'll be fine," she whispered, more to herself than the dog.

Willing the snow to stop, she inched down the road.

Chapter 4

As an outsider watching the proceedings, Sennet wouldn't have picked up on the underlying issues if she hadn't been warned. She wasn't the only human in the room by any means; the elves weren't nearly as strict as they had been before about human lovers, and some of the half-breeds in the audience could have easily passed for human themselves.

Those sitting in the circle deciding succession and the petitioners-- Meinren, Oriellen, and one other elf who Ceidrin named as Ahren--all pled their positions. The only two missing who should have been there, Elinor and Lucien, caused a stir when the names were read, but no one approached the deciding elves to plead their case or give their regrets.

The elves in the circle--all elder, all distantly related to royalty and the prior Queen's closest council--only reacted strongly when Ahren mentioned the possibility Sennet had come up with--that the long-lost princess might have left an heir.

"Oh, now he's done it," Ceidrin muttered under his breath. "He's actually ninth in line to the throne. He doesn't have a chance."

"So you *could* have been up there?" Sennet whispered back.

"No. I gave that desire up a long time ago," Ceidrin said as the murmuring around them rose at Ahren's statement. "But technically, yes. I could be up there." He frowned. "Lucien's absence is particularly damning, since he has had words with both Oriellen and Meinren."

"What about Elinor?" Sennet asked.

"Elinor...Elinor has the blood, but not the status," Ceidrin said. "She spends most of the year in the human realm."

"Perhaps she didn't get the memo," Sennet whispered. Ceidrin laughed.

"All possibilities must be exhausted, or the new king or queen will always have a question of their succession to the throne," Ahren said as soon as the murmuring had died down.

"And are you volunteering to find this missing heir?" an elderly woman asked, her voice sharp. "As far as I'm concerned, we're *already* missing two."

"Aunt Mahariah," Ceidrin whispered, a thread of glee running through his voice. "If anyone could derail this, *she* could."

"I am merely suggesting that the possibility has not yet been raised," Ahren said smoothly.

"And of course I object," Oriellen snapped. "Nidrea has been gone for two *centuries*. Even if she left an heir, a half-human would be dead by now."

"Still, the possibility has been raised," an older elf said, his voice grave. "And this council cannot ignore that possibility."

"You would have the kingdom remain without a leader while Ahren indulges in his fancy?" Meinren spoke for the first time, and Sennet felt something shimmer in his words; some sort of spell, perhaps? She glanced at Ceidrin, who now watched the proceedings with narrowed eyes.

"We've survived for this long while our Queen was ill," Mahariah said, but her voice wasn't as strong as before. And perhaps it *was* a spell, because Ceidrin made a forceful motion with one hand and Meinren stepped back, his face suddenly white.

"Damn it," Ceidrin growled under his breath, then stood. "I agree with Ahren. If there is even a *remote* possibility that Nidrea left an heir, we must explore it."

Sennet thought that Ahren seemed a bit relieved to have his proposal seconded. Oriellen and Meinren could not hide their fury.

"I do not see *you* up here, Ceidrin," Mahariah said, but her tone was not unfriendly.

Ceidrin did not move. "You know why."

"I--" one of the others began, but Mahariah silenced him with a glare.

"Yes, I do," she said. "And your reasons are *not* in question. Will *you* discover what happened to Nidrea and answer the question of an heir? And perhaps gather up Lucien and Elinor as you go along?"

Meinren smirked, as if he expected Ceidrin to refuse, then spluttered when Mahariah mentioned Elinor's name. "She's no Queen!"

"Of course you will," Sennet whispered when he hesitated. "You know you want to."

"I do not!" But louder, he said, "I would be happy to lay to rest the speculations about an heir. And I will do my best to track down Elinor and Lucien as well. However, I *must* have enough time to complete my task."

"Will a month do?" Mahariah asked with a small smile.

Ceidrin ignored Meinren's glare and nodded. "If I haven't found anything in thirty days, then there won't be anything to find."

"Very well." Mahariah turned to the gathered council. "We will rejoin this council in thirty days. All aye?"

There were only two dissenters.

"What now?" Sennet asked as the crowd began to file out of the room.

"Now I have an excuse to leave early," Ceidrin said, not at all upset by the possibility.

Oriellen appeared behind him, her face as cold as ice. She did not speak as she swept past, but Sennet thought the coldness lingered long after she was gone.

"If she becomes Queen--" Ceidrin bit back the words he wanted to say and sighed. "I should at least attempt to explain to Gene why I've involved myself in this before I leave again."

"Be careful," Sennet said, thinking that the easiest way to end such a search would be to eliminate the searcher.

"Oh, I will," Ceidrin said. "Paranoia is my middle name, after all. Shall I walk you home?"

"No, I can find my own way." And anyway, she wanted another glimpse of that sword so she could try to jog her memory again. She *had* seen that sword before.

Somewhere.

Chapter 5

The steady *thump thump* of windshield wipers woke him first; and then the faint thrum of momentum that vibrated through his bones. Edward thought he had enough strength to open his eyes until he tried--and failed--so he lay and listened and tried to figure out what had happened.

He remembered the cold, although it seemed a dim memory now. Or, perhaps, he was frozen still; he couldn't feel anything but the car's vibration. No throbbing pain; no agony. Just a numbness that swallowed him whole.

He thought he remembered headlights, which would explain the car, but he couldn't remember anything else. No sign that he had spoken to the driver, or begged for a ride. Nothing.

Edward tried again to open his eyes. This time, he managed to pry them open, but he saw nothing of the driver in the darkness of the car. The dog had curled up in the small space above his head, a mass of warmth that almost put him to sleep again. He tried to rise, hissed when his hands came in contact with the seat, and fell back down.

It didn't take very long for the pain to swallow him whole.

"You're awake," a voice said from the front of the car. A feminine voice; young, but strained with fear and worry. "Don't try to get up quite yet; I can help you as soon as I find a place to stay, but--"

Edward closed his eyes and tried to shove the pain away. He wasn't sure how badly he was hurt, only that one small movement had awakened a vortex of agony.

Was it all from the cold? Or had she--

"I hit you," the girl said, as if reading his mind. "With my car. I swerved to miss a deer, and you were standing on the side of the road. I'm very sorry."

"You--" He managed that much before his throat locked and forced him to struggle just to speak. "You *hit* me." Why, then, wasn't he dead?

The dog whined and shifted in place. Edward bit his lip to keep from screaming.

"Yes," the girl said. "And I apologize. I couldn't *miss* you. I'm sorry."

Edward knew he should have been more concerned about this, but he couldn't seem to find the strength to care. He tried to inventory his injuries, but *everything* hurt, down to the very tips of his fingers.

Frostbite? Or worse? He managed to move his hand, then his arm, but he couldn't see details in the darkness as a human. That was one small advantage to his wolf form, and almost the *only* one.

At least his fingers still worked; albeit stiffly.

"I'm sorry," the girl said again.

"It's nothing," Edward whispered, almost before he realized he had spoken. He groped for the dog's head, and rubbed the silky fur on her nose. She licked his fingers and thumped her tail against the back of the seat.

"No! Don't say that!" The girl sounded genuinely distressed. "If I hadn't hit you--"

"If you hadn't hit me, I'd be dead by now," Edward whispered, which was probably the truth. "So I think you actually *saved* my life." He opened his eyes, hoping to get a glimpse of her, but she remained hidden by the front seat.

"Oh," the girl said softly, but Edward had the feeling she was talking to herself, not him. "Maybe they won't notice, then. And--" Louder, she said, "Are you badly hurt? I do have a small talent for healing, but I don't dare work without wards, or else I would have healed you back there. I--"

The heat pouring from the vents was not enough to stop a sudden shiver. "You're a witch?" With the last of his strength, he tried to *see* her, beyond normal seeing, but even *that* part of his vision remained dark.

"You sound like you've had bad luck with witches," the girl said, her voice charged with guilt.

"Answer my question," Edward demanded. "Are you a witch? If so, you can let me out here. I'll walk the rest of the way home."

The dog whined, as if disagreeing with him.

"I don't need *you*, either," Edward whispered, but did not pull away when the dog licked his face. He could *feel* that, at least.

The girl took a deep breath. "No, I'm not a witch. At least not in the way I think you mean."

"But you have a 'small talent for healing'," Edward said, and tried to sit up. He almost fainted from the pain, and had to lie there for a moment, his eyes closed. "What are you, then?"

"I could ask you the same question," the girl said after a moment of silence. "You seem to know a bit about magic, at least--"

"You could say that," Edward whispered, unwilling to give her anything more. Who *was* this girl? He realized, then, that he was completely in her power--for better or for worse. Even if she *did* release him, he wouldn't have enough strength to reach his sanctuary before the change came upon him, or he died in the snow.

Perhaps he could use that to his advantage. She wanted a well-warded place, after all, and if she swore to heal him and held true to her word--

"How--how far have you driven?"

Her laugh sounded close to a sob. "Not far. The roads are very slippery, and I didn't want to...I didn't want to hurt you any worse than I already have." Under her breath, she whispered, "I don't want anyone else to die tonight."

Edward shivered again. "*Tonight?* How many people have you killed?"

She was silent for so long that Edward *almost* fell asleep. "I--I haven't killed anyone. But I--if I hadn't--" She sounded very close to tears. "Never mind. I shouldn't be telling you any of this."

"How did they die?" He couldn't tell if he asked the question only to fend off the silence or to learn more about her.

"I'm not sure I should tell you," the girl said. "The least you know the safer you will be. I'm sorry. I'll--I will heal your wounds and then leave you in peace."

"And if those who hunt you find out that you healed me, where will I be then?" Edward asked, taking a guess on the reason for her fear.

"Where were you walking on a night like this?" the girl countered.

Edward closed his eyes. "Home." His feet twinged at the memory.

"And you usually dress like that while walking through a blizzard?"

"This was all I could find," Edward said. He had secrets of his own, after all; secrets he did not wish to share.

"I see," the girl said, and a moment later, Edward felt the car swerve slightly right as she stopped it on the side of the road. "I'm going to turn on the light; close your eyes."

Edward obeyed even before he considered the possibility of what she could do while his eyes were closed. Even then, the press of illumination against his eyelids hurt.

The dog whined again, then barked; the sound echoed through his head.

The girl's breath caught in her throat. "You're--you're *bleeding.*"

Edward nodded, his eyes still closed. "I expect I am." The wetness he felt had to be something other than melting snow and ice; for one, it was actually *warm.* He covered his eyes with one hand before he opened them, but even after allowing them to adjust, the interior of the car was a blur for a long, long time.

When his eyesight finally cleared, he saw the girl for the first time, kneeling in between the front seats, her spiky pale hair not quite covering the tips of her very pointed ears. Her eyes were wide and as green as grass-- something he hadn't seen since the first snowfall some months ago.

"I thought elves couldn't drive cars," Edward said, which was the only thing he could think of to say, given the circumstances. He shifted on the seat, gasped a little as another avenue of pain decided to open up, and touched the worst of the wetness beneath his side.

His fingers came up red. He stared at them, numb, until his hand started to shake, and then he closed his eyes and tried not to think about what would happen when he shifted shape.

"I'm not a full-blooded elf," she said. "My name is Elinor. My mother was an elf. She's the one who died." She sniffed a bit and wiped her eyes. "I usually wear a glamour to tone down my appearance, but--but I--" Her breath caught in her throat. "I'm so sorry."

She touched him, then, and he felt something *shift* between them; a warmth that passed from her hands through his skin, sinking deep down into his bones. It *burned* where it touched, but it wasn't a painful feeling, just uncomfortable.

Edward opened his eyes. "You said--you said you needed wards."

Elinor shivered and nodded, glancing out of the windows only once before dropping her gaze to concentrate on her talent again. "I do. But I don't want you to bleed to death before I find a place to stay. I don't--I don't want anyone else to die tonight."

There *was* a lot of blood. And maybe some of the numbness stemmed from blood loss; Edward couldn't tell.

"What was the last street you passed? Do you remember?"

Elinor's eyes lost focus for a moment. "Oak Hollow, I think."

"About three miles from there is a turn-off; you may miss it if it's covered with snow." Edward closed his eyes again; it seemed easier just to close them and succumb to the steady drag of weariness than to fight to keep them open. "I have a house at the end of that road. It's well-warded." He wouldn't say a word about the lack of electricity or running water. "It's--a stone house. The only one--on the road. My wards will let you pass."

"Who *are* you?" Elinor whispered, but the car started up again a moment later, and he fell asleep before he could even think to reply.

Chapter 6

Ceidrin didn't really want to face Gene's inevitable anger just yet, so he decided to detour to Elinor's mother's house, a place he'd been to only once or twice before. It was a nice long walk through the forest on a well-traveled path; the estates were normally connected with paths instead of roads in Faerie. Visitors usually arrived by magic anyway, but Ceidrin thought he could use the exercise.

It hadn't been *quite* a century since he'd been in the castle. And even the reams of gossip had not escaped his notice.

But no one had warned him about *this*.

He stood at the broken gate and stared at the destruction---the blackened wood; the soot-stained stone---and wondered if Elinor's absence had a more sinister aspect. The house--and it was a mansion, in truth---had been in her mother's family for centuries. When had it burned?

And how? There were safeguards against something like this in Faerie; magic ruled everything, but did not allow for mundane inventions like fire departments. If he sought out Lucien's home, would he find more of the same?

He ventured down the silent path, every sense straining towards the faint hope that there had been survivors. But as he grew closer and saw the scope of the destruction, he knew that the arsonist--and this was no natural fire--had left no stone unturned.

The whole middle of the house lay opened to the elements as if a bomb--or worse--had dropped from the sky. The fire had not spared a single room; broken glass and scraps of parchment littered the grounds; he picked up a heavy skirt, sodden with soot and rain and wondered if its owner lay dead inside the shell of the house.

Or, worse, *outside* of it.

He found her--or what was *left* of her--chained to a stone bench in the gardens, the silver links untarnished by time or weather. With a sort of numb detachment, he gently slipped skeletal wrists out from the shackles and lay the body down across the bench. When the sun broke free of the clouds, the earthly remains of Elinor's mother crumbled into dust, leaving only her blackened gown behind.

Elvish vampires did not burn as well as human ones, he thought, and filed that observation away for later. Only after he'd turned to look at the house again did he realize what this meant. If someone--and he could not help but see Meinren as the villain in this--was murdering the potential heirs to the throne, then *he* was in danger, too.

And so was Gene.

Ceidrin closed his eyes and tried not to imagine what Gene would say when he told him that couldn't come home. Wearily, he cast a finding for the inevitable spell; the maker of this had to have left some sort of alarm behind to catch unwary visitors. Had Elinor been caught by such a trap? He had no idea if she would have burned like her mother; it had been years since he'd spoken to her. He still thought of her as a child, perpetually serious, an exotic blend of what happened when a human wizard married an elvish vampire.

Was her father still alive?

He found the spell, disarmed it, and waited a moment before casting another spell--this one to find any sign of life inside the remains of the building or the grounds outside. This spell was the only warning he had before the hounds attacked; he sensed their presence just as they burst through the remnants of the gates.

They were elvish hounds, lean and long and mottled grey, but they moved with a fluidity that made him wonder if they hadn't been tampered with at some point in their lives. They were also utterly silent; not a single growl between them. If he hadn't cast that spell, he would have been dead before he realized what was happening.

As they approached he retreated up the wide marble stairs that had once led to the mansion's front door. The door hung on broken hinges, and could be blocked against them, but the shattered windows and half-fallen walls would not protect him for long.

And even then, he felt no fear; no thrill of death; no despair. Perhaps he was still numb from the shock of it all; the very openness of treachery where such a thing had always been hidden, before.

The hounds spread out around the base of the stairs, hemming him in, then slowly advanced, tensed and wary for any sign of attack. When the first one lunged, Ceidrin drove it back with spells and wards, but there were *five* hounds. They would break through his paltry defenses eventually; elvish hounds were bred for their stamina.

Had they attacked anyone else? Had Elinor returned home to find her mother dead and the house in ruins, and had these hounds killed her?

He ducked into the gloom of the house, slipping a little on wet ash. The nearest hound lunged at him, but they didn't follow him inside what was left of the building. Short of finding or forming a portal or trying to make his way across the destruction without killing himself, they had blocked his only exit.

And someone *else's* exit as well. At the bottom of a pile of debris--newly formed by the look of it--lay a body.

Or, at least, Ceidrin *hoped* it was a body, since all he could see of it was a foot and part of a leg. He glanced out the door to make sure the hounds had not followed him, then sifted through the pile, tossing stones and charred wood out at the hounds, who were not pleased by how well he managed to aim his makeshift missiles.

At the bottom of the pile, once he managed to remove enough of the debris to uncover most of the body, lay a bruised and bloody elf, his eyes closed, his face waxen and pale under the filth. From the look of it, he'd lain there for a day at the least; his clothing and hair were sodden from the recent rains.

It actually took Ceidrin a moment to recognize him, and when he did, he felt a bit of the tension release from his shoulders. He'd found *one* missing heir--Lucien--and he was, at the moment, alive.

Ceidrin cleared away more of the debris before attempting to wake him. His pulse seemed slow. Shock, perhaps, or the ragged wounds that covered his body, wounds made by *teeth,* Ceidrin realized, and wondered if the hounds' bite carried any sort of infection, like a werewolf's bite. Sennet would be able to tell, but he had no way of contacting Sennet, except--except for the fact that he did.

Gene had asked him on more than one occasion to carry a cell phone for emergency purposes. Ceidrin hadn't seen the point at first, but he did have to admit that they came in handy at times like these where magic fell short.

He glanced at the hounds--they growled at him in return--and dialed Sennet's number.

"I think not," a voice said from behind him--a growling voice, alien and cold. Before Ceidrin could turn to defend himself, a clawed hand tore the phone from his grasp and tossed it away.

There were *four* hounds now, and one...*creature,* too misshapen to be anything but someone's experiment gone awry. It leered at him, but Ceidrin twisted away from its grasp and cast a ward to drive it back.

"I don't know who gives your orders, but--" his voice trailed away.

The creature shifted shape again. Not into a hound, but into a passable imitation of an elf, the only anomaly a certain look in its eyes. This time, it held a tiny crossbow in one hand, pointed not at Ceidrin, but at Lucien, who was just beginning to stir.

Ceidrin stepped in front of its aim. "Stand down," he snarled, his fury both sudden and white-hot.

In response, the creature shot a bolt out of the crossbow, and then three more in quick succession. Ceidrin's anger helped deflect the first two, but the third one found its mark, and so did the fourth one. Not mortal wounds, no, but they drained him of both strength and fury as if they had been poisoned. He stumbled, then fell to his knees.

"A warning," the creature spat, and buried another bolt in Ceidrin's kneecap. "Do not get involved in this."

Ceidrin gasped as the pain uncoiled through his body, freezing both thought and mind in an unbreakable embrace. "You dare--" He touched the bolts--one in his shoulder; one lodged in the bone of that same arm--and tried not to faint.

The creature raised the crossbow and again took aim at Lucien. "This will be your only warning," it said, and pulled the trigger three times. Desperate, Ceidrin threw up his hand--his other arm was frozen now, unmoveable--and poured the last of his strength into a ward to surround both himself and Lucien. He pulled power from the house itself and felt what was left of its structure groan and sway. But the effort left him panting and drained, his vision speckled with grey.

When he could see again, both the hounds and the creature were gone.

He jerked out one bolt and stared at it; a dull, heavy metal that shouldn't have been in Faerie to begin with. Could he *die* from iron poisoning? Would Sennet be able to track his phone call?

Lucien moaned behind him and Ceidrin turned as much as he was able, his vision swimming now; the pain a dull roar in the back of his mind. His last desperate attempt at a ward had worked; none of the three bolts had met their mark. But he still seemed no better off than before.

When Ceidrin tried to speak his name, his teeth chattered together. *Shock,* he thought, feeling as if he watched himself from a distance. *And you're probably going to die from the iron if Sennet doesn't realize you called. You* do *realize that?*

He tried to shut out *that* voice as much as he could, but it wormed its way into his mind. With a strangled oath that never made it past his lips, he tore the bolt from his knee and felt a great rushing warmth spread through his body. Not healing, no, *poison,* and he could do nothing to save himself.

He should have gone home. But if he had gone home, the hounds could have shown up there, and he would have had to watch *Gene* get slaughtered instead of Lucien.

Of course Lucien was still alive--for now--so maybe not.

Ceidrin closed his eyes and slumped back against a pile of rubble. His mind ran in unending circles, refusing to submit even after the darkness rose to carry him away.

Chapter 7

She *did* almost miss the turn off. The snow had blown into drifts around it, but she managed to find a passable path through the mess. With fields and forest on either side, she didn't really have to worry about ending up in a ditch. But the road dipped and the car sank into pothole after pothole; she had to force herself not to glance back at her passenger for fear she'd finally killed him with one too many lurches.

By the time she reached the end of the road and spotted the small house nestled under a canopy of oak trees--a bonus, indeed--her own bones were aching from the repeated impact. She pulled the car up beside the house, taking care to park out of sight of the road. Only then did she turn to glance at her passenger again.

His eyes were open, at least; she could see a faint glitter from reflected moonlight.

"I'm going to turn on the light again, okay?"

It took a moment for him to reply. "Okay."

When she turned on the light, he winced away from the brightness, his eyes streaming tears. The dog squinted at her from its spot beside him, its tail thumping against the back of the seat.

At least it looked like he had stopped bleeding. "When I touched you before--" She tried her best to meet his gaze, but she couldn't help but retreat from the look in his eyes. "Your right leg is broken. And there was some internal bleeding; I'll fix the rest of that when we go inside. And frostbite, of course; I can fix that, too." There were other things as well; the ghosts of old wounds--and the scars--but she decided not to mention that just yet. If she could heal him before she herself collapsed... "You hit your head, too."

He watched her silently throughout all of this, his face blank. "And what--what would you want from me in return for the healing?"

Elinor swallowed hard. She had known he would ask this; he had already shown himself not to be a normal human, if there were such a thing. And she had considered her response all through the silent drive to his house.

"A place to stay for the day and nothing more," she said. "And then, after dusk, I will leave you in peace."

"And what of those who hunt you?"

"They--" She hadn't thought that far. What *if* her aunt's hunters found his house? What if they found traces of her presence--especially back where she had begun to heal him? "They have no reason to search for me near here." She hoped.

He nodded, then, and closed his eyes. "My wards will let you pass. Be welcome in my home."

Elinor glanced out the window. The snow had stopped now, at least, but it was still a long and cold trek to the porch. "May I have your name?" she asked.

He opened his eyes--bottomless pools of murky green--and stared at her for a long moment. "Edward. Edward Lange."

"My name is Elinor," she said, and tried to smile at him. "I can't remember if I told you before."

"You did." He tried to move then or to brace himself for movement, and his face turned an alarming shade of grey. "Perhaps you should--leave me here. I won't--I can't--"

"I'll wrap you in the blanket and drag you across the snow," Elinor said. "Then all we'll have to do is get you up the stairs." It sounded easier than she expected it to be. *First,* she had to get him out of the car.

With his limited help, she did manage to slide the blanket beneath him, and wrap it around his body. She left the car running until she was ready to slide him out; more for the warmth than for anything else, since the journey over the snow would not be pleasant at all.

When she opened the door, he closed his eyes, shivering helplessly as the cold seeped into the car. The dog hopped out on its own and stood there, waiting, as if trusting her to treat its master with care.

Somehow, she managed to slide him out of the car. Dragging him over the snow was a bit more difficult; when she reached the porch stairs, his eyes were half-open, but unaware of her presence. And for a moment, until he took a shallow breath, she thought that she had killed him.

He blinked. "Up. The. Stairs." She could barely hear his voice.

"Yes." Mindful of his injuries--which *she* had caused--Elinor gently maneuvered him up the stairs. Once onto the porch--which was a lot sturdier than it looked--his wards closed around them.

They were good wards, strong and certain in their strength, anchored in the bedrock under the house and--as far as she could tell--impervious to any suggestion that they crumble.

The vague knowledge of the hunters faded from the back of her mind so completely that she had to struggle to connect to them again. They weren't close. Even hunters had trouble on icy roads.

The front door opened at her touch. She looked for a light switch, but found nothing; only after she glanced out into the yard did she realize that she hadn't seen a single telephone pole since she turned off the main road. So. Edward lived without electricity. That was no matter; it only took a tiny scrap of strength to form a light. She pulled him inside, waited until the dog had entered, then closed the door against the cold.

And as soon as her light illuminated the interior of the house, she wondered if she'd brought him to the right place. The windows were boarded up--from the outside--letting only stray beams of moonlight into what would have been a parlor in any other old cottage. The house itself seemed to have weathered the test of time without much trouble, but there was no visible evidence of heat--and the ancient, dusty furniture would not give off much warmth.

Despite that, the house wasn't freezing cold. The stones themselves gave off some sort of warmth, or perhaps the heat came from the wards. Either way, the walls pulsed under her hand when she touched one of the stones.

With the wards in place, she knew her duty: to heal Edward before he died from his wounds. He wasn't awake when she dragged him inside and unwrapped him, and he didn't wake up when the first strains of her talent seeped into his body. She thought, perhaps, that it was better for him to sleep through the healing. She didn't want to see the look in his eyes when he realized how close she'd come to killing him.

With that thought in the forefront of her mind, she pushed everything else away and concentrated on healing.

Chapter 8

Sennet had left the castle with more questions than answers, but she had to keep reminding herself that this was really not her affair. Ceidrin had asked her to come along, not to help him complete his task.

If the treachery he saw from every corner was truly real, there was little she could do about it. Healers were neutral, after all. Sometimes, she despised that distinction.

"Well met," a low voice said from the trees as she walked back along the path.

Sennet stopped. "That all depends on whom I'm meeting," she said evenly.

The voice laughed, a low, musical tone. "I'd really rather not say. Can Healers be hired?"

"Not as such." Sennet tried to see past the leaves, but the owner of the voice remained hidden. "But we tend to watch out for our friends."

"Do you count Ceidrin as your friend, then?" the voice asked. "Because I am fearful of his safety."

Sennet glanced behind her at the path, but there were no evident eavesdroppers. "He *said* he was going home."

"He did not go home," the voice said. "When I saw the hounds--"

"Hounds?" Sennet asked sharply. *"Whose* hounds?"

"I cannot say," the voice whispered. "Please--he is in danger. Can you go to him?"

"I--" Just at that moment, Sennet's phone rang. It was Ceidrin's number, but no one answered when she said hello. She thought she heard a voice, though, in the distance, but the crackle of static drowned out everything else.

"Do you know where I live?" she asked, her voice cold.

"Yes, of course, but I--"

"I want a straight answer," Sennet snapped, angry with all the intrigue and plots. "Ceidrin is one of my oldest friends. If he's dead, I may blame *you."* Surreptitiously, she moved towards the trees, straining to get a glimpse of her informant.

"I had nothing to do with this," the voice whispered. "Truly, I did not."

"If you knew anything about this and did nothing to stop it, then you are as guilty as anyone else," Sennet said. "Tell me your name, so when I find him dead, I can curse it."

She heard a movement in the trees, and saw a shadow--nothing more-- vanish into the underbrush. And then, far off in the distance, something howled.

Hounds, the girl had said. Fearing for the worst, Sennet listened to the static through the open connection, used that connection to pinpoint Ceidrin's approximate location, and *pulled* herself to that place.

The first thing she noticed when she stood on solid ground was the smell--of ash and decay and death; the second, the faint flickering of two lives inside the ruin. She found them both lying in the middle of a sea of rubble, Ceidrin's hand outstretched, as if in supplication, the other elf barely breathing.

"What did you *do?*" Sennet muttered, and knelt beside him. "I left you alone for an hour!"

Ceidrin's eyes flickered open when she touched the bolt in his arm. "Oh. You came."

"Of course I came," Sennet said softly. "I had a warning, although if you hadn't called me, I would have been hard-pressed to find you."

He actually managed a wheezing laugh. *"This* was a warning."

"You could have died from this," Sennet said, wondering if he realized how close he had come. "The bolts are iron, Ceidrin."

"'Could have' sounds promising," Ceidrin whispered. "Don't let Lucien die."

Sennet glanced at the other elf, then reached across Ceidrin's body to touch his hand. She fed enough of her talent into him to stabilize his condition, then concentrated on Ceidrin again.

"I'm going to have to pull out this bolt," she said. "It will hurt."

He didn't scream, but he bit through his lip. "A warning," he whispered, his eyes sliding shut.

Sennet touched his knee. That was the worst wound; the bolt had shattered both bone and cartilage. Even with her help, it would take weeks to fully heal. *If* it fully healed at all. "You're going to walk with a limp for a while."

Some knot of tension left his bearing. "But I *will* walk?"

"You will if I have anything to say about it," Sennet said. "Lie still. I'm taking both of you to my house."

Ceidrin bit his lip. "Will you call Gene?"

"Yes. I'll call him."

"Thank you."

He did not speak again. And by the time she'd transported both of them to her house, set them up in spare bedrooms, and set her talent to work on both of them, he was unconscious.

Which was probably a blessing, since she had to straighten out his leg to try to heal the damage done to his knee, and he wouldn't have lasted through *that* at all.

Chapter 9

Edward opened his eyes to find he lay on the floor of the front parlor, covered with a blanket he did not recognize and weary beyond belief. He lay still for a long moment, trying to remember why he should be so tired, only realizing after he shifted sideways that someone had put a pillow beneath his head and that the floor itself was slightly warm, belying the coolness of the air.

For a long moment, all he wanted to do was curl up under the blanket and listen to the crackle of flames in the fireplace.

Flames?

He *felt* the heat from the fire--a welcome warmth from the cold outside--but there was no smell of burning wood; no smoke. *Spellfire,* he thought, and wondered if he had cast it in his sleep.

But that didn't feel right. He--*his mind flashed through the blizzard, the car; the sound of a voice. The dog.* Edward closed his eyes. "Elinor?"

When she didn't reply, he struggled to sit up, pushing the weariness away. As far as he could tell, the parlor was empty, its dusty furniture showing no sign of Elinor's presence. He used that furniture to help him walk; his left leg was stiff and aching--his mind supplied that it had been broken. It wasn't now.

When he reached the doorway that led into the kitchen, he realized that he could smell something cooking. That scent awoke a monster in his stomach--a yawning chasm that threatened to devour any tiny bit of strength he had mustered for the trip across the room. He sagged against the door.

She had found candles somewhere, or else had filled a myriad of dusty glasses with spellfire; either way, the resulting light illuminated the kitchen and made it into something welcoming, not forgotten. The old cookstove exuded heat that reached out and wrapped Edward into its embrace--he hadn't fired it up in years. Where had she found the wood to burn? Or was this spellfire, too?

A cast iron skillet sizzled on the stovetop--he recognized that, since it had hung in his kitchen since before his curse existed. A smaller pot sat beside it, steaming, and another pot sat behind it, boiling merrily; there were bags and boxes of things he didn't recognize on the old scarred table that had served as both a preparation place and an eating space for many, many years.

The dog lay in front of the stove, drowsing, and her eyes barely opened at his presence.

He knew from experience that there were no stores nearby, and his closest neighbor was miles away. Where had she found the food?

"There's a hunter's cabin not far from here," Elinor said from where she sat at the table. "I took a walk while you were unconscious." She glanced up at him, as if expecting him to protest her use of his kitchen, but he made no mention of it. The tantalizing scents from the skillet and the pot were too strong. "He left some food behind; I figured it would be bad by spring anyway, so--"

Edward sat down so he wouldn't fall over, then picked up one of the boxes on the table. "He left tea?"

Elinor flushed. "No. I found the tea in the car. Your teapot was rusty, though, so I boiled some snow in another pot--do you drink tea?"

"I would if I had some," Edward said. "As you can see, my--my stores are rather low." It was almost a joke, at that, since he *had* no stores. It was a bit difficult to gather them when he spent the majority of the month as a wolf.

"How--" She sniffed, then, and rubbed her eyes. "How do you *live* like this?" She pushed away from the table, and poured hot water into a chipped mug.

Edward waited until he had taken a sip of tea--which did nothing to dampen his hunger--before choosing his reply. "It is the only way that I *can* live," he said, and wondered if it would just be easier to tell her. If she stayed long enough, she would know anyway.

Without speaking, Elinor pushed a bag of something towards him. He smelled smoke--smoke and salt and *meat*. With shaking fingers, he fished out a piece of dried jerky and bit into it. The hunger *roared*.

"There were onions and potatoes and some garlic in the cabin," Elinor said, watching him with an odd look on her face. "So I chopped up everything and it will be ready in a few minutes."

Hot food. When was the last time he had eaten something cooked? He ate another piece of jerky, then another, and washed it down with tea. "And the water?"

"Boiled snow," Elinor said with that same strange look on her face. "I said that, earlier."

Edward closed his eyes. "Perhaps I am not as recovered as I thought." If he had been, he would have been treating her with more suspicion and less acceptance, since he did not know her true motivations. "Did I thank you for healing me?"

"No. Not yet," she said, and a moment later, his stomach cramped when she placed a plate full of fried potatoes under his nose.

He opened his eyes and inhaled the steam, only noticing after he took the first bite that she didn't have a plate in front of her. "You're not eating?"

"I already ate," she said quickly--almost *too* quickly. "And anyway, you--you only have one plate."

How many years had it been since he'd opened that cupboard? He had no idea if she spoke the truth. "Oh."

He watched her, in between bites, as she scraped the skillet out into an empty bag, and then cleaned it with a cup of water and a handful of what looked like sand. She dried it with a scrap of cloth and hung it back above the stove, then stirred whatever boiled in the other pot. By the time his plate was clean and his cup was empty, some of that desperate emptiness had faded from the corners of his awareness.

"What's your dog's name?" she asked.

Edward glanced at the dog, who hadn't moved from her place in front of the stove. "I---I don't know."

"You don't know?" Elinor frowned, and turned back to the stove. "But---"

"We've only just met," Edward said, and realized that wasn't a very good explanation. "She followed me."

"She seems to be very well-trained," Elinor said. "Where did she follow you *from?*"

She followed up that question by ladling some sort of stew into a bowl he did not recognize, and set it in front of him. When she moved to pick up his cup to refill it, he put his hand over hers.

"I did not ask you to serve me," he said softly, ignoring her question.

Elinor hesitated, her gaze flicking down to his hand, then back up to his face. He wasn't sure what she expected to see there, but she did not pull her hand away.

"No, you didn't," she finally said. "And I have no say in how you live your life, but you were starving to death."

She said this so plainly that he shivered, staring down at the bowl full of stew. "It's been difficult to find food this winter," he whispered. "I--usually I can find a rabbit hole or perhaps a deer--but this winter has been brutal."

And it wasn't over yet.

"I don't understand." Elinor filled his cup up with tea again, and then topped off her own. "Don't you have anyone you can call?"

Edward almost choked on a mouthful of stew. "No, not really." he said before he realized that telling her this would awaken a dozen more questions in her mind.

"My *aunt* wants me dead," Elinor said, as if hoping that by giving him a nugget of information, he would give her one of his own.

"And this is related to your mother's death?" Edward had to think about what she had said before; his mind had tucked that conversation into the back of his mind.

"Yes." Now it was Elinor's turn to close her eyes, but only briefly. "I usually go home--to my mother's house--for the winter, but when I arrived, I found her dead. And the hunters followed me here." She turned away again, wiping her eyes. "I couldn't even *bury* her!"

"I'm sorry," Edward said.

"Thank you," Elinor whispered. Edward watched her as she stirred the rest of her stew, then put her hand on the stovetop, which had to be hot; he could feel the heat even from his place at the table. When she lowered the flame and lifted the pot off the burner, she held the pot with bare hands.

Bare hands. He waited, expecting her to scream, but nothing happened. She set the pot down, stared at it, then at him, and rubbed her hands together.

They were unmarked.

"I have--I have a special affinity with fire," Elinor whispered, but Edward had the feeling that this wasn't the *entire* truth.

"I gathered that," he said, remembering the warmth of her spellfire.

She tried to smile. "My father was a wizard." After a moment, she sat down again with a cup of tea in front of her.

Edward nodded and ate more stew--it was really quite good. Much better than he could have *ever* managed himself, even with a store of supplies. When he was finished eating, he drank the rest of his tea and savored the warmth that spread through his body. He had not felt quite so warm in a long time.

"Would you like some more?" Elinor asked. "There's plenty--"

"No," Edward said. "But thank you. That's the second time you saved my life." He tried to smile, but the suspicion had raised its scaly head now, and he couldn't help but wonder what she wanted from him in return.

"You--" Elinor wouldn't meet his gaze. "You've invited me into your home. It's the least I can do." Did he sense a surge of guilt in her voice now? Had she--

Edward stared at his empty bowl, suddenly sick to his stomach. "What did you put in the food?"

She stared at him, her face so still and blank that it seemed carved from stone. "Nothing," she whispered, but from her tone of voice, he could tell that it *wasn't* nothing at all. "I have no reason to poison you, and I haven't. I'd swear--on anything you choose--"

The wards responded to Edward's sudden alarm, and Elinor flinched as if she felt the slow reversal of their welcome.

"Please--I swear." She pushed back her chair, but didn't rise. "I have no reason to hurt you."

"Except, perhaps, for covering your tracks," Edward whispered. "So your aunt doesn't find you."

"If I wanted to kill you, then why would I bother healing you?" Elinor twisted her hands together, her face closed now, emotionless. As if she could not bear to have him guess whatever secret she was hiding. "I would have--I would have saved my strength."

She spoke the truth. Why *would* she have healed him if her intentions weren't pure? And even if they weren't wholly *pure,* she had saved his life. Twice.

Edward rested his head in his hands. "I'm sorry. Call it a century of paranoia, or just my usual run of luck--"

"A *century?*" Elinor whispered.

For a moment, Edward considered denying what he had said, or refusing to elaborate. But she had gifted him of the reason for *her* flight; surely that meant he owed her a story of his own.

"Yes," he said slowly. "A century."

"But you--" She stood then, and paced around the table--not close to him, but everywhere else, touching the hot stove, the chair, the cabinet--as if trying to convince herself that they were real. "You tasted human."

As soon as she said it, she froze in place and covered her mouth with one hand, her eyes wide.

Edward sat very still for a moment, his mind struggling to hear some sort of threat in her words. But she had spoken without thinking, just as he had spoken, and now her eyes--her eyes shone with tears.

"You said you were--" What *had* she said? He struggled to keep both his wards and his voice calm. "Your mother was an elf. Your father was a wizard." She had needed shelter until dusk. Until *dusk.* He remembered that.

And he knew of only one--for want of a better word--*creature* who would need to hide from the sunlight.

"My mother was born an elf," Elinor said, her voice wooden. "Right before she met my father, she was--attacked. By a--"

"Vampire?" Edward asked, his voice matching hers in tone.

She flinched, despite his efforts. "Yes. My father saved her life."

"I see," Edward said.

Elinor shivered. "My father died a year ago, and I inherited his house. But I always joined my mother for the winter, and I was on my way to do that when I found her." She squeezed her eyes shut. "They burned her house down, too."

"And is *your* house in danger?" Edward asked.

"I--I don't know," Elinor replied. "I didn't know where to *go*. They were right behind me, and I just--just ran away." She buried her face in her hands. "I still don't know what to do."

"Why was she killed?" Edward asked.

Elinor sighed. "Because my mother was related to royalty, the Queen is dead, and I'm now fourth in line to the throne. Although technically, depending on whom you ask, I'm farther back than that, since--" She sighed again. "It's complicated."

"I--" All at once, Edward wasn't sure what he wanted to say about that. "I see."

She managed a watery smile. "It doesn't help that I'm blind in the sunlight," she said. "I have a pair of glasses, but I tend not to need them in Faerie, and I didn't bring them with me."

"So you *can* go out," Edward said. "In sunlight, I mean." Sunlight was a vampire's main adversary, at least as far as he knew. He thought, perhaps, that being a hybrid would be an advantage instead of a drawback.

What, then, were the *dis*advantages?

You tasted human. He heard her voice in his mind.

"You're half human," he said slowly. "So does that mean you--you have to drink someone's blood to survive?" By the flush on her cheeks, he knew he'd hit fairly close to the mark. "You drank *my* blood?"

"Only enough so I could finish healing you," Elinor whispered, staring at him as if she expected him to drive her out at any moment. "I've been driving all night, and before that--before that--" Her face crumpled, and she turned away. "I'm sorry. I never meant for any of this to happen."

Edward's lips twitched. He couldn't help it. She was the picture of misery, a waif, lost and alone, but she had no idea-- "You said I tasted human."

"You did," Elinor said, her voice firming when he didn't order her out. "Well, mostly, at least. I thought you weren't, at first, but--"

"I'm not," Edward said. "At least not anymore." He decided not to tell her about his mother, or the fact that he'd never been wholly human.

"I don't understand," Elinor said. She wiped her eyes, still standing on the other side of the table. "I'm sorry."

"You said I tasted human," Edward repeated, not quite knowing how to tell her. "If you had tasted my blood tomorrow, you would have tasted wolf."

Chapter 10

Ceidrin awoke with a gasp, his mind only half-believing that he lay safe in Sennet's house and that the blankets covering his body--and the fact that he was still alive--was not some strange sort of dream.

He moved his arm first, hesitantly, and it responded with only a small amount of pain. That was encouraging, considering he hadn't been able to move it before.

But when he tried to move his leg--

"Don't get up," Sennet said from the doorway. "And I don't want to see you *try* to put weight on that yet."

Ceidrin sank down into the softness of his pillows and closed his eyes. "They've crippled me," he whispered.

"They would have if I hadn't found you," Sennet said, and he caught the scent of mint tea from the tray she carried. And then, almost casually, she asked, "Where was Gene supposed to be today, Ceidrin? Do you know?"

Coldness settled in his chest and constricted his throat. He stared at her, his eyes wide. "He's not home?" *Would it be too much to ask to keep him out of this?*

"He's not answering the phone," Sennet said. "With your permission, of course, I can go check on him." Her voice and manner suggested that she would hate to find the worst-case scenario, and Ceidrin did not even want her to suggest it.

"Please," he whispered. "I've not been gone for weeks, only a handful of days. He lives his own life. He could--just--be out."

"Then stay in bed," Sennet said. "Drink your tea. I'll be right back."

She left the mug on the table beside his bed and helped him sit up, but he had no stomach for tea at a time like this.

"Under *no* circumstances do I want you to stand up, okay?" Sennet asked. "I couldn't heal all of it. Not now. When the tea I gave you earlier wears off, it's going to hurt."

"You gave me tea earlier?" Ceidrin asked. He didn't remember anything after her arrival at the burned out house.

"You were unconscious," Sennet said. "But I'm serious, Ceidrin."

"Is Lucien alive?"

"Yes. He's asleep, and he won't wake up before I get back." Sennet smiled at him, but the smile never reached her eyes. "Do I have to make you promise me?"

"No." Ceidrin couldn't find enough strength to smile back at her. "I'll stay right here. I won't move. Just--please. Find Gene."

So the coldness of panic would go away, and he could concentrate on healing.

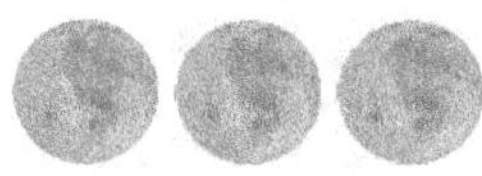

Sennet left the house with a heavy heart, not at all wanting to discover what she thought she would find when she arrived at the house Ceidrin and Gene shared. It was an odd little house, hand-built and sheltered by a grove of trees, anchored in wards and surrounded by meadows. Gene's garden sprawled across what would have been lawn in any suburban setting, but it was winter now, and the snow covered everything.

The snow also made it more difficult not to leave tracks, but she saw nothing amiss as she approached, save for a small package lying on the doorstep, innocuous in its innocence.

Gene's little car sat in the driveway, cleaned off, not covered in snow. There was no sign of a struggle or anything else as she walked up the cleared path to the door.

She picked up the package as soon as she reached it. It had Ceidrin's name on it--his *full* name, not the one he used in the human realm--and it had no return address.

And then, almost out of the corner of her eye, she saw that the passenger side door of Gene's car wasn't closed all the way. Holding the package, she veered away from the front door and walked down the path to where the car sat.

She couldn't see the ground until she grew closer; the snowbank on the side of the driveway hid it from view. But as she approached, she saw the first signs of trouble--a bunch of celery, now brown and wilted; a bottle of something--wine?--and a host of other groceries lying scattered across the driveway.

From the look of it, the groceries had been there for at least a day, maybe more. The eggs had cracked and frozen in slimy streaks across the asphalt; something had dragged away a package of meat and devoured half of it. But there was no sign of Gene at all.

Sennet carefully set the package on the bench beside the door, and walked to the side door, stepping over broken bottles and quite a few packages of ruined fresh fruit and vegetables.

The screen door was closed, and so was the door beyond. *Both* were locked, but with Ceidrin's permission to enter, Sennet didn't need a key anyway, so she opened the doors and stepped inside.

She'd always rather envied Gene's kitchen. It wasn't very big, but it had enough storage to put most kitchens to shame. He had an ancient, cranky stove that he loved, an equally ancient fridge--bright blue--and a stained glass window over the sink. What was there *not* to love?

The house, however, was empty and silent. Sennet sensed no sign of life, save for a lonely betta in a sparkling clean bowl. Even then, she searched the entire house before reassuring herself that Gene was not there.

She almost would have rather found him lying in a pool of blood--still alive, of course--than conspicuously absent.

Did the *package* have something to do with that?

Sennet fed the fish, locked the door behind her, and picked up the box again. It was damp on the bottom, of course, from where it had sat on the wet concrete, but it wasn't heavy or ticking or anything like that.

She opened it carefully, poised to neutralize a spell, but the box only contained a small leather bag, worn and supple. Inside that leather bag was a folded piece of paper, a lock of dark hair and a ring--twin to the one Ceidrin wore.

Sennet unfolded the paper and read the contents with a frown.

Do not get involved in this. If you do, your lover will die.

How had they acted so quickly? Both Oriellen and Meinren had been at the gathering, and Ceidrin had been attacked an hour after the council disbanded. No one had known that Ceidrin would volunteer to search out Nidrea and the others; *he* had even professed that he wished he had not come.

But from the look of the groceries, Gene had been snatched *before* the meeting. Not afterwards. Had they taken him as collateral, just in case?

Perhaps *knowing* that Ceidrin couldn't stay uninvolved?

Sennet transported herself back to her house, then, since there was no trail to follow. She gently laid the leather bag back in the box, then carried it to Ceidrin's room.

And hesitated outside the door. What could he do but worry and fret and curse his kin until he drove himself crazy? It would be more of a kindness not to tell him and let him heal.

But she couldn't keep so terrible of a secret to herself. Not without destroying their friendship when he discovered she had lied to him.

Sennet opened the door and stepped inside. Ceidrin's smile of welcome fell from his lips as soon as he saw the expression on her face.

He closed his eyes--to steel himself, she thought--and took a deep breath.

"Is he dead?" His voice cracked on the last word.

"Honestly? I don't know," Sennet said. "But he was taken, and his kidnappers left you *this*." She held out the box.

With shaking hands, Ceidrin opened the leather bag and emptied its contents in his lap. His breath caught at the sight of the ring more than the lock of Gene's hair.

But when he raised his head after reading the note, Sennet saw only fury in his gaze.

"They--"

"Who are *they?*" Sennet asked.

Ceidrin threw the box on the floor. "My *cousins*. Oriellen and Meinren, I'd guess. One warning was not enough?"

"They took Gene at least a day ago, maybe longer," Sennet said. "I think they knew you'd get involved." She told him about the groceries, and watched the color leech out of his face.

"Damn them."

"Is there anything I can do?" Sennet asked. "To get him back? Anyone I can talk to?"

Ceidrin buried his head in his hands. "No. Short of finding a way to heal me faster, so I can kill them both--"

He was, she thought, absolutely serious. That was the scary part. She had never seen him like this before. But then again, no one had ever kidnapped his lover before, either.

"Your knee was shattered," she said. "Elves heal quickly, but not *that* fast. And you know the rules."

"I know. You can heal the wound, but not give me back my strength." Ceidrin growled something under his breath. "I can't do *anything* from a sickbed."

"You can tell me where to look," Sennet offered.

"Healers are neutral, and this is not your fight," Ceidrin whispered, and closed his eyes. "How bad would it be if I walked on this?"

"It might not fully heal," Sennet said. She'd expected that question before, when he first awoke. "You could-- potentially--limp forever."

He kept his eyes closed, as if he didn't want to see the expression on her face. "Could you--could you make it strong enough for me to walk? I'll use a cane if I have to, for the rest of my life if I have to, but I can't--I can't leave him there, Sennet."

"Only if you let me help you," Sennet said. "Tell me about these hounds. Surely your cousins themselves did not shoot you."

"One of the hounds shifted shape," Ceidrin whispered. "It--I had no idea they could do that. It took away my phone, and shot me. As a warning." He opened his eyes finally, and stared at her. "It had every intention of killing Lucien."

"He wasn't shot," Sennet said. "He had quite a few broken bones and a lot of other wounds, but he wasn't shot."

"I warded us both against the last three shots," Ceidrin said. "I didn't think it would work."

And he didn't seem to realize how remarkable that was in itself. "You warded yourself against *iron?*"

A slow smile spread across his face. "Yes. Yes, I did. Desperation does amazing things, doesn't it?"

"Just as long as desperation doesn't get you killed," Sennet said. "Now. You had to have some idea as to where Nidrea ended up or you never would have volunteered to find her heir."

"I know where she ended up," Ceidrin said, and leaned back against the pillows again. "I spoke to her once, almost a century after she ran away. We--ran into each other by accident." His eyes slipped shut. "She swore me to secrecy, and you are the only person--other than myself, of course--who knows."

"Did she have any children?" Sennet asked softly.

Ceidrin grimaced as he shifted position a bit. "A son."

"Older than Meinren?" Sennet asked.

"Yes, by at least fifty years if he's still alive," Ceidrin said. "And by default, he would be the heir even if Isabel left one."

"Because Nidrea is the elder sister," Sennet said, nodding.

"Do you have any more of that tea?"

"It will put you to sleep," Sennet warned.

"At the moment, falling sleep is the only way for me to see Gene again," Ceidrin whispered. "Will you heal me?"

"I'll do my best," Sennet said. "And I'll find you a cane to help you walk."

"Thank you."

He was asleep by the time she returned with the tea, but she helped him drink it anyway, and then set to work on repairing his knee as much as she could.

She owed him that much, at the very least.

Chapter 11

Elinor stared at him with her mouth half-open, gaping like a fish. "But...the full moon's tonight," she said, not understanding. "You *can't* be a werewolf--"

He closed his eyes, and she wondered if he had intended to tell her anything at all, at first. "I'm not." The smile fell from his lips. "My...my curse is just the opposite. The moon's still full, at least until dusk, and I'll remain human until then. But after that, I'll be a wolf, unless I have enough strength to fight the change for a day or two."

Something changed in the way he held himself as he said this; some invisible string of tension finally snapped. He took a deep breath, let it out, and then stared at her, slightly challenging.

"And--" Elinor did a rapid calculation in her head. "You're only human during the full moon? For the past *century?*" Which meant a little more than three years as a human, and more than ninety as a wolf. She had wondered why he lived without any modern conveniences; without any stores for the winter, in a dusty old house that had never seen the advent of electricity. Now she knew. How could he plan any sort of life around *that?*

"Yes." With obvious effort, he stood and slowly walked back into the parlor. When he returned, he held a small, framed photograph in his hand.

She took it from him and stared down at a faded portrait--a young man dressed in a sober suit, unsmiling and stiff. Even with the passage of time and the addition of scars, the young man was very obviously Edward Lange. "You weren't born this way, I presume?"

"No." He took the picture back without looking at it. "I was cursed. By an--an elf. A witch." He limped back into the parlor, carefully placed the photograph back in its place on a bookshelf, and sank down into a dusty chair. "Winter's the worst time of the year. Game isn't as plentiful as it used to be, and I--I'm tired."

Elinor followed him, but stopped in the doorway, not wanting to intrude on what seemed to be such a private sorrow. He wasn't accustomed to visitors, or speaking; it was almost as if he had forgotten her presence.

"You said you were walking home--from where?" she asked when the pall of silence became too thick for her to stand.

Her question startled a laugh from his lips. "I--I tried to go farther afield last month. But I killed the wrong chicken, I guess, and the people who lived at the farm called the--the authorities. I spent two weeks in a cage until the moon allowed me to change, and then I left. The dog--the dog came with me." His face turned bleak in an instant. "That's the first time I've eaten well all winter long. And I wasn't sure what I'd find when I came back here."

"You were trying to walk home from the city?" Elinor asked. It had taken her hours to get out of the city--in a *car*.

"I don't think they had taken me that far," Edward said, and stood up again. "If you don't mind, I'd like to change my clothes before...before it's too late."

Before he *couldn't* change them, Elinor realized. "Go ahead," she said, her throat dry. "It's *your* house; I'm just a guest here, and nothing more."

How had he survived for so long? Alone? Perhaps the witch he'd mentioned had been an ill-fated request for help. Surely he had to have tried to break the curse over the years--and even more surely, he had probably given up.

She watched as he limped through another doorway, leaving her alone in his refuge--and the place that might one day become his grave. She hadn't healed his leg completely; her talent wasn't strong enough to mend broken bones without a single trace. Had she helped him at all, or just prolonged the inevitable?

His wards wrapped around her as she walked through the downstairs, peeking into dusty rooms that held echoes of long ago eras. The boarded up windows only let in thin ribbons of sunlight; not enough to hurt, but enough to see by.

There were three other rooms--a library crammed with books, another parlor, and what had probably been a scullery off the kitchen back in the time that the house was last in the present and not stuck firmly in the past. It hadn't seemed right to explore before. It didn't seem right now. But she couldn't sit still.

The house was full of oddments---a strangely familiar sword peeking out of an umbrella stand, a collection of dusty rocks that sparkled when she picked one up. There were other photographs, and even a painting of a gray-eyed lady hanging over a small table in the hallway.

She ended up back in the first parlor, on a chair that was probably antique and worth a decent amount of money, considering its age and condition, no closer to a solution than she had been before.

When Edward appeared in the doorway wearing jeans and a long sleeved black t-shirt that only accentuated his pallor, Elinor knew that she had to make sure the hunters never caught wind of his involvement. He didn't deserve to be caught up in her mess.

His feet were bare. He followed her gaze, smiled, and shrugged. "It's harder to find shoes that fit than it is to find clothes. I'm still working through a bag of clothes that I found on the side of the road last spring."

"What will happen tonight?" Elinor asked before she could stop herself.

Edward sat down in the same chair. "I don't know," he said. "I used to fight the change. And maybe manage to stay human one or two more days and nights. Sometimes--sometimes even close to a week. But I haven't fought in a long time, and it was difficult even then."

"Why didn't you...surely there's some way to feed yourself, especially in the wintertime. You could go to a store--"

"And steal?" Edward asked with a small smile. "I feel badly enough about the things I have stolen already."

"Oh." She hadn't realized how hard it would be. Without money. Without help.

Edward pulled out a pair of crumpled bills. "I stole these," he said. "Thinking that I might--" He favored her with another small smile. "I thought that if I could make it to a store, I could--perhaps--buy food enough to last the month, but I can't quite bring myself to buy--" He let the money drift down to the floor. "It is no matter now. I wouldn't have been able to carry anything home as it was."

"But you...you can't just give up," Elinor said. "I can buy you food with the money you have. I'll drive to the nearest grocery store when the sun sets and bring back enough food to last--" And she *could* do it, too. But how would he keep the food from spoiling? How would he open cans as a wolf? Short of buying a really big bag of dog food--

"I had thought there might be food for...for pets," Edward said softly, as if he could read her mind. "But that seems more akin to giving up. And I can't--quite--bring myself to do that." He hesitated. "Yet."

Elinor shook her head. "No. I would call that *survival*. Sometimes...sometimes you do what you have to do, and damn your pride."

"I do have to feed the dog, if she's staying," Edward said. "And I don't think the witch who cursed me expected me to survive this long." He hesitated. "Where will you go from here?"

It was a blatant attempt to change the subject, and at first, she was tempted not to let him get away with it. "I don't know," she said. "My mother has family in Faerie, of course, but some of that family are the ones who murdered her. I don't know who I can trust. Not anymore." When he didn't reply, she pushed on to break the silence. "I have a cousin who lives here in the human world, but I haven't seen him in years."

"You should get some rest." Edward yawned, then shook his head, as if to shake the weariness away.

"Do you want some more tea?" Elinor asked.

"No. I *want* to sleep. But I...I don't sleep when I'm human." He sighed. "I try not to, at least."

"What would you be doing if I wasn't here?" She asked the question before she realized what the answer had to be. Without food, provided he could have made it back to the house, he would have been dying. Starving. Alone, with no strength for spellfire or anything else.

Edward met her gaze. "I wouldn't be here," he said, and hunched over in the chair, covering his face with his hands.

Had *she* done this to him, somehow? Had she made it worse by helping him? "I'm--"

"No. Stop apologizing," Edward snapped, the first sign of actual anger she had seen. "This is not your fault, and not your affair." He stood, swaying slightly, and averted his gaze from her face. "I need...I need to be alone."

Elinor nodded. "Of course. I'll just...I'll stay in the other parlor until dusk, and then I'll leave you in peace." Her chest felt tight; she wanted to help him, but she also realized she had no claim on his time or how he lived what life he had. If he wanted to give up, then who was she to stop him? He'd been living like this for a *century*.

Blindly, Elinor left the room and crossed the wide foyer to the other parlor. This one was smaller, but no less dusty, and the sofa's rusty springs poked through the faded upholstery. Elinor chose a small loveseat as her bed, cast spellfire in the tiny fireplace to warm the room, and curled up under a velvet quilt. Only then, after she'd cast all thought of Edward from her mind, did she allow herself to fall asleep.

Chapter 12

Ceidrin awoke to find a wooden cane propped up against his bed, another mug of tea--piping hot--on the table beside his bed, and even a change of clothes folded neatly at the end of his bed. He drank the tea first; if only to steel himself for disappointment if his knee would not hold, then threw back the covers and slowly stood up.

He had to grab the cane to keep from falling, but he managed to stay on his feet. His knee ached--his whole *body* ached--but it was a manageable pain.

And one he would learn to live with, if he lived *through* this.

Perhaps he had erred in keeping Nidrea's secret for so long. At the time, he'd seen no harm in it; her sister was Queen and would be queen for many years to come, and Oriellen and Meinren had not yet begun their plotting to take the throne. No one had ever asked him if he'd seen her in his travels, and he had not volunteered the information.

He sat down on the bed and laid the cane across his lap. It had a silver band around the top, and when he twisted it, he unsheathed the sword hidden inside--a thin, rapier-like blade that shone in the dim light.

"I thought that might come in handy," Sennet said from the doorway. She held a tray in her hands, with more tea and some sort of sandwiches, which she set on the end of Ceidrin's bed.

Ceidrin smiled. "Yes, if I can manage to unsheath it and stand at the same time." He put the sword away and stood up, finding his balance easier now than before. "You--um--you're determined to help me? Despite the fact that they might try to kill you, too?"

"I'm determined to help you so you can get Gene back and survive this," Sennet said. "Healers aren't very easy to kill. But we're *very* good at uncovering secrets."

"I can tell you where Nidrea lived a century ago," Ceidrin said, and took one of the sandwiches. "But if you go there and do not find her--"

"Where are *you* going?" Sennet asked, a trifle sharply. As if she had guessed a bit of what he planned to do.

"Back to Faerie," Ceidrin said, and stared down at the sandwich in his hand. "The only person I am certain that I can trust is my Aunt Mahariah, and *someone* else needs to know what happened, just in case I fail."

"And your cousins won't expect you to go back to the castle and tell on them?" Sennet asked.

Of course they would. But what else could he *do?* Sit here and wait until the succession was announced, then slink away like a beaten dog? "I could--" He stopped, then, as a terrible thought swam to the forefront of his mind. "I have no way to free Gene, save for one that I can think of," he whispered.

"What is it?" Sennet asked when he didn't continue.

Ceidrin closed his eyes. "If I went to them--my cousins--and gave them the information I'm about to give you--"

"And if they decide you'd be better off in their dungeons?" Sennet asked. "What then?"

"I don't think they would kill me," Ceidrin said, but he knew he didn't believe his own words. They had killed Elinor's mother, after all, and maybe even Elinor. And they had almost killed Lucien. "And I have to believe they haven't killed Gene. Because if he is dead --" his voice rose, "I would murder both of them and damn the consequences."

"I know you would," Sennet said softly.

"I have to try," Ceidrin whispered. "I can't just leave him there and let them have the crown. Not anymore."

"I have a better idea," a voice said from the hallway. Lucien limped into view a moment later, and leaned against the door, spent and weary. Privately, Ceidrin thought he looked no better than he had before, but at least he was conscious and mobile now.

"You should be asleep," Sennet said, but her voice held no heat.

"I heard you talking," Lucien said. "And I rather wanted to know what happened. You saved my life?"

"Ceidrin saved your life," Sennet said. "I healed you."

"Then, thank you, Cousin." For a moment, he seemed at loss for words. "I...I owe you my life."

"I have no desires for the crown," Ceidrin said. "And I could not leave you to die."

"Ah, yes. The crown. But surely--"

"They raised the question of your whereabouts, and the succession was postponed for thirty days," Ceidrin said. "Elinor is also missing. And I was *supposed* to search out any possibility of Nidrea having an heir--"

"Nidrea?" Lucien stared at him in shock. "But--" He smiled, then, and shook his head. "I would have seen Elinor as Queen before Nidrea's name was mentioned."

"Ahren mentioned it first," Ceidrin said. "Well, Sennet mentioned it first. But they've murdered Elinor's mother, and perhaps even Elinor--"

"She was alive," Lucien said. "And I don't think they caught her." His face darkened. "I wasn't in any--condition--to warn her when she arrived and found her mother dead."

"What were *you* doing there?" Ceidrin asked.

"I--I wanted to speak with Elinor before the gathering. To warn her," Lucien said, but something rang false in his tone of voice. As if he'd intended to do something more as well, like ask her not to come. "But I found the house in ruins, and her mother dead. I was attacked--"

"By the hounds Ceidrin mentioned?" Sennet asked.

"Yes." Lucien rubbed his arms. "Are they--*infectious?*"

"I don't think so," Ceidrin said. "I think whoever they belong to made them that way. They aren't werewolves."

"But they shift shape, don't they?" Lucien asked. "I--I remember seeing *something--*"

"They shot at us with iron," Ceidrin said, and told him the rest of it as well, just to see his reaction. His voice caught a little when he spoke about Gene, but he managed to keep calm enough until the end. He said nothing about Nidrea's son, or his promise to her, since Lucien had seemed so surprised to hear her name.

"That's why I said I had a better idea," Lucien said. "I understand you want your--your lover back. But they won't give him to you until the succession is assured."

Ceidrin knew he spoke the truth, but he still didn't want to hear it. He closed his eyes, as if to block out Lucien's words. "Then what do you suggest?" he asked, his voice harsh. "You don't even know what information I intended to give them!"

"Give them my death," Lucien said softly.

Ceidrin stared at him. "What?"

"You aren't the only one they've--harmed in this," Lucien said. "If they believe I am dead--if *everyone* believes I am dead, even if only for a little while--"

"What does that gain *you?*" Sennet asked.

"It gives me leave to be invisible, in a way," Lucien said, and that thread of *something* ran through his voice again. "I have my own score to settle with our cousins."

"If I tell them you are dead, they'll want proof," Ceidrin said, wondering what sort of score Lucien had to settle. "And I have no proof to give."

"And that other information you intended to tell them?" Lucien asked. "I have to assume it had something to do with Nidrea--do you have proof for that as well?"

"No. But I expected they would truthspell me on it," Ceidrin said, and nearly shuddered at the thought. "And I can tell them that with the utmost certainty of truth."

"You must truly love this human of yours," Lucien said softly. "To submit yourself to something like that--"

"I do," Ceidrin said.

"What did you intend to tell them?" Now there was only curiosity in Lucien's voice; nothing more.

"That I met Nidrea--by accident--a century ago, and that she introduced me to her son," Ceidrin said. "And that she invited me to her home, and swore me to silence. And I have held onto that silence since that day."

"Nidrea--" A bottomless sorrow had opened up in Lucien's gaze. "Nidrea is dead. I didn't know of her son."

"You sound as if you have personal knowledge of her death," Sennet said when Ceidrin did not speak.

Lucien held onto the doorway as if it were the only thing holding him upright. And perhaps it was; his skin was now tinged with grey. "It is my fault she is dead," he whispered. "Isabel sent me with a message for her sister some time ago. It took me a long time to find her, and I did not consider that someone would follow me."

"How long ago?" Ceidrin asked.

"Fifty years, perhaps," Lucien said.

"Fifty years ago, a half-breed wouldn't have even been considered for the throne," Ceidrin said for Sennet's benefit. "Times have changed."

"Especially since one of the contenders is a half-vampire," Lucien said. "If Nidrea's son still lives, then he would be king. There would be no question."

"I'm not going to pretend to understand the complexities of elvish law, but who truly has the closest chance if Nidrea's son is dead?" Sennet asked.

Ceidrin and Lucien exchanged a glance.

"Truly?" Lucien spoke first, his gaze on Ceidrin. "Succession doesn't normally move from sister to sister, or sister to sister's son. If a king or queen dies without heirs, then--normally--their branch of the family never regains the crown."

"But this is not a normal situation," Ceidrin said. "Isabel died by deceit."

"If Nidrea had no heir, if her son is dead, then in all usual circumstances, the crown would fall to the eldest child in the various branches of the family closest to the throne. Not aunts or uncles, but the eldest *child*."

"And who is that?" Sennet asked patiently.

Ceidrin cleared his throat. "That would be me," he said. "But I renounced my standing a long time ago. I have no--"

"You may not have a choice," Lucien said. "They may try to take it by force, Ceidrin."

"They already have," Ceidrin whispered. "They've murdered Isabel, almost crippled me, and came very close to killing you. They've killed Elinor's mother, and I'm sure they are chasing Elinor even now. If Nidrea's son still exists, he doesn't have a chance. They don't care about the normal ways of succession."

"And yet you were willing to give him up to them?" Sennet's voice held no reprimand, but Ceidrin flinched anyway.

"I was willing to tell you the location and hope you got there first," he said, still staring at Lucien. "In the hope that they would release Gene and let me go on with my life."

He said this without much hope or belief, because he knew they wouldn't let him go. Not now. And maybe not ever. Was Gene already dead?

"There is one way you can end this," Lucien said into the silence.

Yes. Assume the crown. Ceidrin almost laughed, but shook his head instead, still silent.

"And if Ceidrin dies? Who is closest, then?" Sennet asked.

"If Nidrea's son is dead and Ceidrin is dead, then the crown would be mine," Lucien said. "After me, then Meinren. Then Elinor."

"In the normal course of things," Ceidrin whispered. None of his bright ideas had come to fruition at all. He closed his eyes and tried to think. How could he--

His hands found the lock of Gene's hair. *A lock of hair.* They had given him something exclusive to Gene; a token, of sorts. Which meant, since he presumably had the rest of his hair in its proper place, that he *might*--possibly--be able to circumvent their spells and find out--at the very least--if he was still alive. Then he could plan his course of action.

"Sennet, I need a bowl of water."

"You've thought of something?" Sennet asked.

"I thought of a way to see if Gene is alive, at least," Ceidrin said, and used the cane to help him stand. "Or if you have something better in mind than a bowl of water--"

"I have a television," Sennet said. "And a mirror large enough to open a portal if that's what you want to do."

Ceidrin hadn't considered opening a portal. But snatching Gene out from under their noses would definitely put them on the defense.

"Can you get through their spells?" Lucien asked.

"I don't know," Ceidrin said. "But I can try. There *are* rules, after all, and we aren't at war. Yet." He tried to keep his voice under control; it might not work, after all, and becoming too excited about it wouldn't help the eventual disappointment. "Let's use the mirror."

"Then follow me," Sennet said, and led the way down the hall.

Chapter 13

Despite his words, he fell asleep anyway, curled up on the loveseat beside the fireplace. When he awoke, the silence in the house felt different--more *empty,* if there could be such a thing. When he slid off the loveseat, he walked on four feet instead of two.

Sunlight no longer streamed through the cracks in the boards covering the windows. Instead, the night outside was clear and cloudless, illuminated by the almost full moon--his time for freedom had passed.

He was a wolf again.

With only a twinge from his back leg, he padded through the house, but the only sign he found of Elinor was a folded quilt in the other room, and two skillets full of steaming food on the kitchen floor. The jerky and the rest of what she had found were in easy reach; he wouldn't starve to death for a while, at least, but he wasn't hungry yet.

The car was gone, too, and so was the money he'd dropped. But she'd left a note on the front door, stuck to it by magic, written in a neat, precise hand.

I left at dusk. I'll bring back food, and then be on my way. I know you said to stop apologizing, but I'm sorry. I'm sorry for everything.

--Elinor

He remembered what he had said to her, and wondered if that had been the weariness talking, or if he truly wished to die. After all this time, it seemed stupid to give up, despite the fact that he had no true hope that he would ever be free of his curse.

Edward turned away from her note and padded back into the kitchen. The food still sat within easy reach. It hadn't vanished. Feeling slightly ashamed of himself for thinking it would, he returned to the parlor and lay down in front of the fireplace.

Only then did he remember the dog, and realize that a presence had been watching him from the shadows since he awoke.

He raised his head and found her almost at once, watching him, her eyes wary.

But she had seen him shift shape before--so why the wariness now? Edward stared at her for a moment. Could they *communicate?* He'd never really tried.

Can you hear me?

The dog's head snapped back as if he had struck her. She growled, her fur bristling, then shook her head, as if to cast out his influence from her mind.

My name is Edward, Edward said silently. *I mean you no harm.*

The dog bared her teeth, then, as if reminding herself that he hadn't harmed her yet, pushed back. It was a formless push--a question more than anything, but he didn't understand it.

Not yet, at least. With practice, who knows?

What is your name? Edward asked.

The dog puzzled over this for a moment, and then gave him a picture of a flower. It took Edward a moment to identify it; he had no use for flowers as a wolf, and even less use for them in human form.

Rose?

She wagged her tail and wiggled all over. More pictures ensued--a bombardment that Edward raced to understand. He saw a man--tall and dark and kindly who had given her treats and taken her for walks in the forest-- and then, a prune-faced woman who had locked Rose in a little room before two other men had taken her away.

Is your master looking for you? Perhaps Edward could ask Elinor to find the man, and return Rose to her rightful home.

Sorrow. A picture of raindrops on a window. Her closest approximation to tears, Edward supposed. She didn't seem to have any trouble understanding his questions at all, which was strange. All the other dogs at the animal shelter had been mindless--or, if not mindless, then frightened and scared.

Is he dead? Edward asked.

Rose whined, confused. And perhaps--just perhaps dogs didn't have a word for death.

How did you escape the cage? Edward asked.

She sent another picture of her master sitting in what looked to be a library with shelves of books Edward would have liked to read. He was showing her something--a trick that wasn't a trick; human magic that a dog should not have been able to perform. She'd tried it in the room the woman had locked her in, but the trick only worked on mundane locks, not magical ones.

Her master had been a wizard, of course. Did the pets of wizards somehow absorb some of their humans' talents?

Edward's sole interaction with a wizard had been Arthur Caswell, the man who'd moved in next door some sixty years ago. But he'd been dead for twenty years, and his ghost had not seemed to want to stay behind.

You can stay here, Edward told Rose, who watched him carefully. *If you want to.*

Sunshine. A cat to chase. A clear pool of water. Bones. Rose grinned and wagged her tail.

Evidently, that meant yes.

Edward closed his eyes and concentrated, then, on *that which made him human.* It was easier to do this when the moon was almost full; he'd never tried to shift shape during the new moon and he doubted it would work. But now, now, he shifted between wolf to mostly human, and staggered to his feet a moment later.

"Elinor is bringing back some food," he said to Rose, who approached him for the first time, her head down low. *Submissive.* Was he her master now? "Do you need to go out?"

She wagged her tail again and beat him to the door.

Edward remembered to slip into his only coat and jam a hat on his head before venturing out into the cold. Even then, he stood and shivered as she finished her business, staring out at the snow-covered darkness. When Elinor left--

He didn't want to think about what would happen when Elinor left. She could just as easily never *return.*

He stood still and let the power of his wards soak into his body; tested the line of them for any sign of sabotage. He felt--*something*--a flicker, quickly gone--to the east, but he could not find it again, and he found no sign that his wards had been breached.

That was where Arthur's house had once stood, just beyond the expanse of his land. Edward frowned. Could a ghost be summoned by a single yearning? Or was it something else entirely; even Elinor?

Rose raised her head and looked at him, and for a moment--one very *small* moment, since he doubted his leg would hold--he wanted to shift shape and join her out in the snow. Just forget what he was and what he'd have to do to survive the rest of the winter, and *play*.

And then, the moment was past, and she stood in front of him, her tail wagging, an image of contentment in her mind.

With one last wistful glance at the snow, Edward turned to walk back into his house, into warmth and the embrace of his wards. Perhaps Elinor would return soon, and then he could--what?

Rose sent him an image of an outstretched hand.

"Why would she need *me* to help *her*?" he asked, and stopped in front of the painting of his mother.

Despite his heritage, he had not gotten involved in the concerns of Faerie, save for that one small interaction with the elvish witch that had left him cursed. He wasn't sure he wanted to get involved with them at all, much less in something that concerned a crown.

His mother had never been very enthusiastic about crowns.

Chapter 14

Sennet's mirror was nearly as tall as she was, and set in a plain wooden frame. It seemed out of place in a room that also housed a television and an overstuffed couch, but Ceidrin wasn't about to say anything about her decorating attempts. He knew she didn't particularly care.

Without asking, she provided him with a candle and a flame to light it; after that, it was only a small bit of magic to ignite a few strands of Gene's hair and gift his name to the mirror. After that, circumventing the spells that surrounded his presence, and not setting off any alarms was a matter of skill more than talent.

The mirror shimmered, casting Ceidrin's reflection--and that of the room beyond--into shadow.

"Can you create a portal without an alternating mirror?" Lucien asked as Ceidrin tried to coax some clarity from the darkness. Was that a *wall?*

"Of course not," Ceidrin said. "If I made a portal from here, it would only go one way. But I can make one from a puddle of water, or a doorway, or anything else that comes to hand to get back out once I find him." *If he could push his way past their spells.* It was hard enough to do that right now, on the opposite side of their defenses. And how long would it take them to notice his presence before they attacked?

"Careful," Sennet warned as his concentration slipped. She extended her hand and touched the surface of the mirror, her face intent on something Ceidrin could not see. "We need a bit of *light.*"

The room beyond the mirror brightened just enough for Ceidrin to make out a figure slumped against the wall. He could not definitely identify the figure as Gene, but he saw no one else in the room, and he'd spent enough time nestled against his lover's body to know every inch of him.

He stepped back, almost overbalanced, and caught himself against the mirror's frame. "You're not going to try to talk me out of going through?"

"Can you get back?" Sennet asked, quite seriously.

Ceidrin opened his mouth, then shrugged, staring at the silent figure lying beside a seeping stone wall. "I'd have to open the door," he said. "There's not enough water in that room to form a portal."

"I'm not sensing a single thing from inside that room," Sennet said. "It could be illusion; it could be Gene. Are you willing to take that chance?"

Lucien stepped up behind them. "I'll go in your place."

"You'll do no such thing," Ceidrin said calmly. He tried to think of another alternative, but other than carrying in the way out..."Sennet, do you have any other mirrors?"

"One," Sennet said, "but I don't think you could carry it and walk at the same time, Ceidrin."

He hadn't thought of *that.* "Damn."

"Then let me come with you," Lucien said. "I'll carry your mirror; you see to your--your human. We'll leave together. All three of us."

"You'd throw your lot in with *me?*" Ceidrin asked. He still wasn't certain about Lucien or his loyalties; his branch of the family had always been a bit close-mouthed and quiet.

"You could end this in an instant," Lucien said softly. He truly did not look as if he had enough strength to lug a heavy mirror a matter of inches, much less feet.

"And when they kill me, what then?" Ceidrin asked. "They'd just pick us off one by one until there was no one left to deny them the throne."

"You could--"

"Without proof?" Ceidrin asked, knowing what Lucien would suggest even before he finished. "Then I would not be a king; I would be a tyrant."

Lucien closed his eyes and rocked back on his feet. "I wanted to speak to Elinor because I had every intention of asking her not to come," he said. "I thought she was in the least danger of all of us, and if they tried to do something at the gathering, then at least one of us would be free."

"And?" Ceidrin asked when he didn't continue.

"I am not aligned with our cousins," Lucien said. "I would prefer to see the true heir assume the throne. And if that means helping you find out if Nidrea's son is still alive, then so be it. But if Nidrea's son is dead--"

"Why don't you find that out first before deciding what to do about it?" Sennet suggested. "The longer you stand here, the closer you are to discovery. Do you want to try to use my other mirror? Or should we circumvent any possibility of a trap?"

"How do you propose to do that?" Ceidrin asked, hating the fact that he felt so helpless.

"Healers go where they are needed," Sennet said, and touched the mirror again. It shimmered, then solidified into a portal. "Lucien, stay here. Keep the portal open."

"You can--you can *do* that?" Ceidrin asked, following Sennet as she stepped through.

"Of course," Sennet said.

"Why didn't you suggest that before, then?" Ceidrin limped over to where Gene--hopefully--lay against the wall and fell to his knees, unmindful of the filth underfoot. He caught his breath as a bolt of pain shrieked through his leg.

"I felt that," Sennet said as he reached out his hand for something to hold onto before he collapsed.

His hand found bare skin, both bruised and bloody, and then the body awoke under his touch--flailing and cursing in a broken voice that Ceidrin instantly recognized.

Using both his hands, forgetting about balance and the screaming pain in his knee, he gathered Gene close and held him until he stopped struggling.

"Hush, hush, you're safe now," he whispered, his fingers trailing across unfamiliar wounds as Sennet's talent worked its magic. "What did they *do* to you?"

Gene sagged in Ceidrin's arms, suddenly limp.

"It's more like what did they *not* do to him," Sennet murmured. "But..."

"Ah, no," he whispered, stricken. "No. No. Tell me they didn't--"

Gene went rigid in his arms. He would have screamed, Ceidrin thought, but his voice had given out a long time ago.

"Hush," he said again. "Gene, it's me. Ceidrin. I swear to you--you are safe now. I won't let them hurt you again."

Gene's hand slowly reached up to touch Ceidrin's face."Ceidrin?"

"You're safe," Ceidrin repeated.

"They...they told me you were dead--"

"I very nearly was," Ceidrin said, and tried to stand up, forgetting about his knee. He lurched forward, instead, and had to bite back a scream.

"What part of 'be careful' don't you understand?" Sennet snapped. "Hold still, both of you!"

Ceidrin laughed. It was either that or sob. "Gene, you remember Sennet."

Gene's arms quivered as he pressed himself against Ceidrin's chest. "How could I forget S-Sennet?"

"She's here to help, so tell her anything you might need," Ceidrin said. "I--I can't carry you out of here; I'm sorry. I was wounded, and I--"

"The heads of the elves who stole me away, for starters," Gene said, his voice suddenly cold. "But I know you can't give me that."

"You're right," Sennet said. "I can't give you that. But I can heal your wounds--"

"Not all of them," Gene whispered.

"No, not all of them," Sennet said. "Some you'll have to heal yourself. Ceidrin might be able to help you with that."

"They--" Gene's voice cracked and he clutched at Ceidrin even tighter than before.

Ceidrin's entire leg was a mass of pain now, but he didn't dare shift position. "Whatever they did can be undone," he said, and hoped that were true. "When I found out you were gone, I thought--I thought I had lost you forever. My cousins can be cruel."

Sennet stood, and gently disentangled Gene's arms from around Ceidrin's chest. From somewhere, she produced a blanket, which she gave to Gene to cover himself. "Can you walk through the portal by yourself?"

"I think so," Gene whispered.

"I thought Healers were neutral," Ceidrin said, which was something he'd wanted to say since she told him she would help him. "Isn't this a bit--not neutral?"

"Healers may be neutral, but we aren't stupid," Sennet said. "And you're my friend. We tend to take very good care of our friends." She helped him up next, and let him lean on her all the way back to the portal.

"I think I may need a crutch after this," Ceidrin said through clenched teeth, but Sennet did something with her talent that took away some of the pain. By the time he stepped out of the mirror again, he thought he might survive.

Gene stood in the middle of the room, clutching the blanket around his body, shivering, even though it was quite warm in the room. Ceidrin ignored Lucien in favor of leading him to the couch and sinking down beside him as Sennet closed the portal.

"Will you be okay?" he asked softly.

Gene shuddered. His dark hair covered the expression on his face, but he twined his fingers through Ceidrin's, as if unwilling to release him. "I think-- maybe. Yes. They--" His breath caught in his throat. "Do you think I could have a bath?"

"Of course," Sennet said. "I would rather you not go alone."

Ceidrin's thought he saw the flicker of a smile on Gene's face before it vanished again. "I would rather not *be* alone," he whispered.

"Then you shall not," Ceidrin said, and with Sennet's aid, helped him down the hall to the bathroom so he could wash the marks of his ordeal away.

Chapter 15

Elinor couldn't quite bring herself to buy the biggest bag of dog food she could find--for Edward, at least. She grabbed a bag of the least offensive brand for the dog, but Edward deserved something other than mere survival, despite the fact that he had been a wolf when she awoke that evening.

So she bought two of the biggest steaks she could find, bagged everything up, and drove back to his house, half-expecting the wards to deny her entry.

There was sign that *someone* had gone out; the footprints of a dog or a wolf in the snow. But both Edward and the dog--the former in human form--were inside when she opened the door; Edward lying in front of the fire, his legs outstretched, and the dog beside him, her head lying on his stomach in a perfect picture of contentment.

They both seemed to be asleep, although the dog's ears swiveled at her arrival.

Elinor took that moment to study Edward in more detail. Something about him--some feature of his face, or the way he moved, perhaps--struck her as familiar, but she could not place the feeling with anything concrete.

And perhaps it was the curse; since it was Faerie-made, that could very well be the familiarity. If the woman whose painting hung in the hallway was his mother, then he resembled his father more. Shaking her head, she carried her bags into the kitchen, poured a bowl of food for the dog, and set to work.

The dog arrived in the kitchen twenty minutes later, looking hopeful, and Edward followed behind her, hesitating in the doorway.

"I bought food," Elinor said when he didn't speak. "And more tea."

"Rose says thank you, and so do I," Edward said. "I--I wasn't sure you'd come back. I'm sorry for doubting you."

"The dog's name is Rose?" Elinor asked, and received a happy bark for her trouble. "You've--"

"Spoken?" Edward smiled. "Yes. We've spoken. In a way. Her--master was a human wizard. I think he's dead, but she doesn't have a word for what happened to him. She thinks in pictures."

"Oh," Elinor said. "I'm sorry, Rose." She didn't have much experience with pets; her father had a cat who hated her, and her mother had never kept a pet in Faerie. "Did you see my note? I thought you'd find it there--"

"I saw it," Edward said, and glanced away from her. "But why should you take the time to help me? You have no reason--"

"Maybe I just wanted to help," Elinor said, but she couldn't find any heat to back up her words. "I'm sorry. I just don't know what to do or where to go next."

"Did you sense the ones who hunt you while you were out?"

"Not a sign of them," Elinor admitted. "My aunt could have called them back, but I don't know. She doesn't give up easily."

"Maybe they got picked up by the dog warden," Edward said with a straight face, and after a moment, she realized he had meant that to be a joke. But even as she realized that, she couldn't help but try to imagine it, and the look on Oriellen's face.

She laughed. "That would eliminate the problem, wouldn't it?" she asked. "But I have a feeling they'll be back. To pull them off my trail means they were put on someone else's, and there are plenty of others who are in danger because of this."

"Is there no one neutral you can turn to?" Edward asked. "Even if just to ask advice?"

"The only true neutral parties anywhere are Healers," Elinor said. "But I'm not sure they could help me with this. They're not into successions, really."

"It wouldn't hurt to ask," Edward said. "And aren't *you* a healer anyway?"

Elinor felt herself flush. "Not like they are," she said, and busied herself at the stove. "I only have a small talent for healing." She tried to sound as if that didn't really matter, but it did. She had small talents for *everything*. Almost.

"Will you tell me more about the succession?" Edward asked, and poured himself a cup of tea. "I think I'm involved now whether you want me to be or not." He hesitated. "And maybe I can help."

Elinor's first impulse was to refuse; to deny him both an explanation and his offer to help. But she also realized that by having him as an ally--even in the form of a wolf--she would have something her cousins couldn't touch. She doubted very much that anyone could get past his wards if he didn't want them to.

"I would be honored to have your help," she said, and meant every word. "But are you certain you want to get involved? They...they burned down my mother's house and murdered her. And they would have murdered me if I hadn't run away."

"There are other heirs?" Edward asked. "Other than you, I mean?"

"Yes. My cousins Ceidrin and Lucien are actually before me," Elinor said. "But the succession is--complicated." She didn't know every detail of the whole story, but she knew enough to tell him. "A long time ago, the heir to the throne ran away with her human lover. She abdicated, I guess, leaving her sister Isobel to rule when their parents died."

"Isobel was the queen who recently died?" Edward asked.

"Yes." Elinor poured herself a cup of tea, then put both steaks on a plate. She set the plate in front of Edward, then sat down across from him. "She was probably murdered. I don't know for sure, because I don't actually *live* in Faerie. And I only heard about her death a few days ago." The message had come from her mother, a carefully worded letter that appeared in her mailbox. "Isobel left no heirs, though."

"If Isobel left no heirs and your aunt is next in line--"

Elinor smiled as he took a bite of steak. "It's actually a bit more complicated than that," she said. "The succession doesn't usually go from sister to sister, or even to sister's son. There are three or four branches of the family that kind of take turns."

"But your aunt and cousin don't want to take turns," Edward said.

"No, they don't." Elinor briefly closed her eyes and tried not to see her mother's body in her mind's eye. "They want the crown, and they will do anything to get it, I'm afraid."

"Who is the *real* heir?" Edward asked. He'd finished one steak already, and started in on the second after giving Rose a nice big chunk. "Who has the most claim?"

"Well, that's where it gets complicated," Elinor said and laughed. "Because there's a cipher--if Nidrea had any children, then her children would be heirs by default."

Edward almost choked on his supper. *"Who?"*

For a moment, Elinor thought he would say something else, but he bit his lip and glanced down at Rose instead. "Isobel's sister--the one who ran away--was named Nidrea."

"And if...if N-Nidrea had no children?" He asked this in a whisper, his hand shaking as he raised his cup to his lips.

"Are you okay?" Elinor asked.

Edward pasted on a smile. "I'm fine. Just a little tired, I think."

He wasn't very convincing, but what could she do but believe him? "If Nidrea had no heirs, then Ceidrin would be the first choice, since he's the eldest of us all. The crown always goes to the eldest child, unless my aunt manages to change that. I know she wants to."

"She wants the crown," Edward said. "And if she doesn't get it, she wants her son to have it."

"Exactly." Elinor watched him for a moment more, but he seemed calmer now, as if the surprise at hearing Nidrea's name had passed. Maybe he had heard it before, however far-fetched that may be. "And if no one is available to contest her will, she'll get the crown."

"What would stop her from killing anyone who gets the crown?" Edward asked, his face still a bit pale.

"That's why I don't want it," Elinor said fiercely. "I don't want her to have it either, but--" She sighed. "Maybe I should contact the Healers. Or my cousin Ceidrin, since he's in danger, too."

"Is he the one who lives here?" Edward asked.

"Yes, with *his* human lover," Elinor said. "I've only met them a couple of times. But he'd probably talk to me."

"If your aunt hasn't already killed him," Edward said.

"True." Elinor sighed. "Do you have a better suggestion?"

Edward hesitated. "Perhaps. Let me see what I can find you to eat, and have a look at something I saw just before you got back. Okay?"

"You don't have to--" Elinor began.

"If we're going to be partners, then you need to keep up your strength as much as I do," Edward said. "Is animal blood okay?"

Rose raised her head at that, but made no sign she understood the word.

"Animal blood would be preferable," Elinor said. "I don't usually--um--drink--"

"I'll be right back," Edward said. He pushed back from the table, stood up, then shifted shape in one fluid moment.

"Thank you," Elinor said awkwardly.

Edward the wolf gave her an unreadable glance, then slipped out the door.

Chapter 16

"Do you know why Ceidrin doesn't want to be king?" Lucien asked after Ceidrin and Gene vanished down the hall.

"I would assume it has something to do with Gene," Sennet said, and noticed how hollow-eyed and weary he looked. "Why don't we go eat some lunch and discuss it? You look like you could use something to eat."

"I'm--" Lucien closed his eyes and pinched the bridge of his nose. "Food would be wonderful," he said. "Thank you."

"And then, perhaps, you should get some rest," Sennet said. "I healed your wounds, but I can't help you regain your strength." She took his arm as he stood and swayed, but he managed to walk to the kitchen under his own power.

Once there, she fixed them both egg salad sandwiches and sat across from him at the table while the water heated for tea. "Why doesn't Ceidrin want to be king?"

"When they--Gene and Ceidrin--first met, certain members of his branch of the family tried to bribe Gene to leave him," Lucien said. "There was an--

argument. Almost a battle, really. And Ceidrin left. It took him about thirty years to set foot in Faerie again."

"Does that have anything to do with why Gene doesn't seem to age?" Sennet asked. She'd always wondered about that, but hadn't felt it her place to pry.

Lucien finished the last of his sandwich without replying, then sighed. "There are ways to ensure humans don't grow old," he said. "It creates a sort of bond between the elf and the human; that's why they're usually lovers. It's not done very often."

"And I assume it doesn't protect them against accidents or sickness," Sennet said.

"You would assume aright," Lucien said. "I'm not...I'm not well-versed in humans. And I think our next king or queen *should* be."

"Would you like another sandwich?" Sennet asked. "And some tea?"

Lucien hesitated, then nodded. "Please," he said. "And thank you."

"Tell me about Oriellen's hounds," Sennet said, and poured him a cup of calming tea. "Ceidrin said one of them shifted shape."

"All I know is that they appeared and attacked me," Lucien said, his voice low and weary. "I've not seen them before. If Oriellen has been running her own hunt, she has been very circumspect."

"And their mistress?"

"She will not stop until she has the crown," Lucien said. "I didn't realize the depths of her desire, before. But now I know."

A shadow in the doorway alerted Sennet to Ceidrin's presence; he looked both preoccupied and tired.

"Gene fell asleep," he said before she could ask. "I thought I'd come and get something to eat before I went back to him."

"I wouldn't leave him alone for long, if I were you," Sennet said. "But you have time to sit and eat a sandwich. Would you like some tea?" She wanted to tell him what she'd seen when she healed Gene's wounds; what they had done to him, but that would have to come from Gene himself.

"Yes, but I can get it myself," Ceidrin said, and did just that. "And I have no intention of leaving him alone for long. A nap sounds like a great idea right now."

"You still need to tell me where you saw Nidrea last," Sennet said, "so I can start searching." When he opened his mouth, perhaps to refuse or to declare his intention of going himself, she shook her head. "Don't even think about it. I can take care of myself, and Lucien knows where she lived, too, remember?"

"Do you have a map, then?" Ceidrin asked with bad grace. He limped to the table, pulled out a chair, and sank down, frowning. "I'll show you where her house was. But I...I owe you enough already, Sennet. You don't have to do this."

"I will go," Lucien said.

Ceidrin took one look at him and shook his head. "No."

"But I--"

"You look like hell warmed over, to use one of Gene's phrases," Ceidrin said. "Get some rest. Sennet can go in search of Nidrea's heir."

Lucien thought about protesting; Sennet saw the words die before they reached his lips. "Is there another bed I can sleep in?" he asked.

"Third door on the left down the hall," Sennet said. "Go to sleep. Ceidrin and I can handle this part."

Lucien left, looking all too pleased to do so. Ceidrin watched him go, then turned back to his sandwich. "You could have--"

"*You* agreed to let me help you, not Lucien," Sennet reminded him.

"Do you have a map?" Ceidrin repeated.

"I have a mirror," Sennet said, and produced a small round mirror from a nearby drawer. "You can show me where it is." She set the mirror up in front of him. "All you have to do is touch it and show it what you see in your mind."

"And then you'll magically be able to go there?" Ceidrin asked. "This is--"

"Yes," Sennet said, which eliminated the rest of his protests. "We might not have much time. If either Oriellen or Meinren discover that Nidrea had a son--"

Ceidrin shuddered. "I pity him, then," he said. "Very well." He closed his eyes and touched the mirror's glass.

A road appeared in the mirror, a winding country road with field and forest on either side. In Ceidrin's memory, it was summer, and the corn stood green and tall while the leaves on the trees had yet to turn their various colors in their autumn display. There were houses here and there, spaced far apart, isolated and alone like little islands amid a sea of green.

Down a winding gravel road was a small stone house surrounded by oak trees, a picture-perfect cottage whose tiny yard bloomed with flowers. It was a peaceful house, a perfect place for solitude--or exile.

It looked very familiar, but Sennet couldn't get a fix on it at all. She frowned. "Was it well-warded?"

"Of course," Ceidrin said, and opened his eyes. "If you were a runaway heir to a throne, wouldn't you ward your home?"

"I can fix on the road--the first one--but anything after that is blank," Sennet said. "Were there any houses nearby?"

"I have no idea," Ceidrin said. "Nidrea didn't inform me whether or not she had neighbors. I was there for an hour at the most."

"Wait--" Sennet touched the mirror and the little stone house vanished. Half a mile away, across a field and a stand of trees, now covered in snow, she saw the remains of another little house, un-warded, abandoned and cold.

"This is real time?" Ceidrin asked.

"Yes," Sennet said, and watched as a wolf--or at least it *looked* like a wolf--appeared out of the fuzzy grayness that were the very active wards around Nidrea's former home and picked its way across the snow.

Towards the trees and the other house.

"Hmm."

"You've thought of something," Ceidrin said, staring at the wolf.

"Yes, I have." Sennet shrugged into her coat and found a hat after a bit of rummaging in the hall tree. "Will you rest? And stay inside? I'll be back as soon as I can."

Ceidrin watched her, his expression both weary and worried. "Be careful," he finally said. "We'll stay here. And I promise to get some rest."

"There's food in the fridge if you get hungry again," Sennet said, and focused on the wolf's destination; the house amid the trees.

When she opened her eyes, snow crunched under her feet and the searing cold tried to freeze her lungs. She stepped up onto the sagging porch, glad of her coat now that she had arrived. It only took a bit of talent to cast a warming spell across her skin, and she waited in comfort for the wolf to arrive.

It slipped out from the shadows a moment later, its eyes catching the reflection of the moon with an odd green glow. It stood and stared up at the house for a long moment, and then--and then shifted shape. In the wolf's place, a young man stood, his dark hair hiding the expression on his face.

He shivered, glanced back at the barely visible stretch of road, and took two steps before he sensed Sennet's presence.

Before she could speak, he growled something under his breath. Sennet felt something *flex* around her; some sort of ward, she thought, and made sure her hands were in full view.

"I mean no harm," she said softly, knowing he could hear her. "My name is Sennet, and I am a Healer." He seemed strangely familiar, as if she'd healed him before a long time ago. And perhaps she had. "Do you know the person who used to live here?"

The young man stopped his careful retreat and stood there, just looking at her, for almost a minute before he spoke. "His name was Arthur Caswell." Each word was measured carefully before leaving his lips; Sennet could feel his distrust like a living thing around her.

And that was why this place seemed so familiar. "Arthur. Oh, yes. I've been here before."

Now it was his turn to study *her*. "You have?"

"A long time ago," Sennet said. "And that's the reason why you look so familiar. Arthur called me one day--you'd been shot. By a hunter, I think." *And he hadn't aged a day since she saw him last,* Sennet thought. How long ago had that been?

The young man touched his stomach, right where Sennet knew there would be a scar. "I don't remember you," he said. "Why are you here? Why now? Arthur's been dead for years."

"I'm sorry to hear that," Sennet said. "How did he die?" She remembered Arthur Caswell as an older gentleman, yes, but in good health. How many years ago *was* that? She couldn't remember.

"I--" The young man scowled. Sennet didn't think he had given her his name before; from what she remembered, he had barely spoken at all. "How do I know you are who you say you are?"

"May I have your name?" Sennet asked. "I gave you mine, after all."

For a moment, she thought he'd refuse, but then he nodded, jerkily. "My name is Edward. Edward Lange."

"And you live in the stone house that sits behind those wards?" Sennet asked. Fifty years ago, according to Ceidrin and Lucien, Nidrea had been living in that house, alive. When had she died?

Edward took a step back. "You...you've seen my house," he said flatly.

"I've been inside your house," Sennet said. "To heal you. Do you remember?"

He glanced away, his gaze shadowed. "Thirty years ago. I don't remember you, but I remember the hunter. I remember that I was dying." He spoke in a monotone, all emotion gone from his voice. "Arthur had gotten past my wards somehow. He had seen my house. And I was hunting on his land when the hunter shot me."

"And then he called me," Sennet said. "I can prove to you what I am if you still don't believe me, but I would have to touch your hand."

He stepped back, even though he was not within reach. "Why are you here?"

"I came here to help a friend of mine," Sennet said, wondering how much she should tell him. "His name is Ceidrin, and--"

He reacted to that name by retreating even further, poised to flee. But then, he wiped his hands across his face and shook his head, as if trying to convince himself to stay. "I...I expect you'd be happy to know that Elinor is safe, then," he whispered.

Sennet saw raw fear in his gaze, and wondered what she had done to make him so afraid. "I'm very glad to hear Elinor is safe," she said softly. "But I did not intend to upset you. I'm sorry. How long have you lived in that house?"

He closed his eyes, then, and braced himself against something she could not see. "My whole life," he whispered. "I was born in that house."

"How long ago?" Sennet asked. Was *he* Nidrea's son? Was that even possible?

He glanced away. "I was not born with the form of a wolf. That happened when I was eighteen."

"Arthur didn't tell me anything about you," Sennet said. "Only that you needed my help." She stretched out her hand. "Edward, I'm not here to hurt you."

He stepped closer; that, at the very least, was progress, but he made no move to touch her. "I could go back," he whispered. "Behind my wards where you cannot go."

"Is Elinor behind your wards?" Sennet asked. "Is she okay?"

"I told her I would bring her back a rabbit or something," Edward said. "So she could eat."

"Then do so," Sennet said. "Don't let me stop you."

That startled a laugh from his lips. "You want--"

"I am here to do one thing," Sennet said. "To ensure that if Nidrea's son still lives, he has not been found by those who would wish him dead."

He flinched at the name, and glanced back towards his house, as if longing to return to the safety of his wards. "Elinor told me what happened," he said. "Did you find her m-mother?"

"Ceidrin did, and almost died because of it," Sennet said. "But he's safe now."

"Elinor was planning to contact him," Edward said. "She--" He covered his face with his hands, then, and sank down into the snow. "She doesn't know."

Sennet couldn't leave him kneeling there in obvious pain, even if his pain had nothing to do with an actual wound. She inched down the stairs until she stood a few feet in front of him, then held out her hand again.

"I mean you no harm."

He raised his head. "I know you don't. I can--*feel* what you are." He hesitated, then took her hand, and Sennet helped him back onto his feet.

"You were wounded recently," she said. "Who healed you?"

"Elinor did," he whispered. "She--" He glanced back again, and shivered. "She hit me. With her car."

"She *hit* you?" Sennet did not stop him when he slid out of her grasp. "Elinor is a Healer?"

"She says not like you," Edward said. "It's...it's a long story. I suppose--"

"How long have you lived--"

"I was cursed one hundred years ago," Edward said quietly. Up close, she couldn't help but see the torment in his gaze. "One hundred and *eighteen* years ago, I was--not entirely human, but close enough."

"Your father was human," Sennet said. "If you are who I think you are."

"I am a wolf except for a handful of days before and after the full moon," Edward said stiffly. "I can't do what you are thinking. I can't."

"What am I thinking?" Sennet asked. She certainly wasn't going to push him; he'd vanish into his wards and close himself off from everyone again.

"Elinor said that if Nidrea left an heir--"

"I'm a neutral party to this," Sennet said gently. "I'm not about to kidnap you and force you to do something you don't want to do. That's not the way Healers work." When he didn't reply, she said, "But I would like to speak with Elinor. No one told me she was a Healer." And if she had enough talent to heal the wounds she'd sensed, she had enough talent to ensure herself a place anywhere for the rest of her life.

"I don't want to be involved in this," Edward whispered.

"Was Nidrea your mother?" Sennet asked.

He blew out a breath, took a step backwards, and started to shake his head. "Even if I lie to you, you already know the truth," he said. "Yes. Nidrea was my mother. And Elinor doesn't know."

"She may need to know," Sennet said. "May I cross your wards?"

His breath caught in his throat. "You...you may. But I told Elinor I'd bring her something to eat--"

"I'll wait here, then," Sennet said. "We can go back together."

From the look in his gaze, he didn't think that was any better than the alternative, but he nodded, shifted shape, and loped away into the trees.

Sennet sat on the edge of the porch and stared across the snow-covered field. What was already a complicated situation had suddenly become much worse. The elves might have accepted a half-human king, especially if he was proven to be Nidrea's son, but she doubted they would accept one who was a wolf for most of the month.

How had he been cursed? Who had cursed him? And could such a long-standing curse be broken?

She would have to find out.

Chapter 17

Perhaps it was the fact that he had a full stomach now, but Edward found it quite simple to find and subdue two rabbits for Elinor. Hunting them kept his mind off the Healer and what would happen once she followed him to his house. Or what would happen afterwards.

For a moment, as he stared at her from the shelter of the trees, he wondered if he could get away with vanishing back behind his wards, closing himself off from everything, and forcing Elinor to go with her, perhaps, and leave him alone again.

Until the next snowstorm, when he would run out of food and eat the wrong chicken and perhaps die this time instead of finding a way to escape their cages.

He stepped out into the open and saw Sennet straighten up.

"You came back," she said. "I wasn't sure you would."

He had said something similar to Elinor, and *she* had come back. "I said I would let you through. And I will." He raised his hand to show her the rabbits. "They aren't getting any warmer."

In human form, it was a longer trek across the snow, and colder, too. By the time they reached the edge of the wards, Edward was beginning to wish he hadn't left his coat behind.

"Here--" Sennet touched his arm before he could pull away. "I can give you warmth."

She did something, then, that sent a tingle of magic across his skin. And suddenly, he wasn't cold anymore.

Edward blinked. "Thank you." He hesitated. "I was walking home when Elinor hit me. If I had this--*warmth*--then, I think I might have made it home."

"Where were you walking *from*?" Sennet asked.

"Ah--" Edward laughed. It *was* a bit amusing, now that he could look back on it. "It's been a bad winter. It's been hard to find food. And I--um--ate the wrong chicken."

"Oh, I see," Sennet said. Her voice sounded a little funny, but she didn't laugh.

"I got to eat for two weeks, at least," Edward said, and tried not to make that sound as hopeless as it actually was. "This might be a silly question, but are you bound to tell them anything?"

"I'm not bound, no," Sennet said, and Edward had a feeling that she'd expected him to ask that question before. "Healers cannot be bound. But Ceidrin visited your house once, when your mother was alive. He may not accept word of your death if I lie to him."

"I can't be king," Edward said, and tried to ignore the fear that threatened to swamp him with that one little word.

"No, I'd say you can't," Sennet said. "Not if you're a wolf for most of the month. How were you cursed?"

Edward stopped right outside of the circle of trees that surrounded his house. "Arthur didn't even know *that*," he said, and shook his head, trying to dislodge the long-ago memories of that terrible night. "I told Elinor that a witch cursed me. An elvish witch."

"And was that the truth?" Sennet asked.

"Most of it," Edward replied, and started walking again.

"The elf who cursed you--do you know who she was?"

Edward snorted. "She didn't stop to give me her name." She hadn't stopped to do much, but murder her prey and then turn her wrath on him. "I...I interrupted her hunt."

"In the human realm?" Sennet asked, and he heard the surprise in her voice.

"My mother was an elf," Edward reminded her. "Elinor said that her cousin Ceidrin--your friend--lives here with his human lover. So it must not be *that* remarkable."

"But a *hunt?* That's a bit--obvious, here. No one hunts in the human realm unless they want to keep something secret."

"Then perhaps this elf wanted to keep her hunt secret," Edward said. "She was hunting a werewolf. When I...when I intervened, she killed the werewolf and hunted me instead." They had arrived at the house finally, and Edward touched the stone beside the front door, giving his wards Sennet's name and declaring her as much of a friend as Elinor.

For now, at least.

When he opened the door, Elinor appeared in the doorway of the parlor, her eyes widening when she saw Sennet behind him.

"Elinor, this is Sennet," Edward said, and held out the rabbits. "She's a--"

"A Healer," Sennet said. "And so, I gather, are you."

Elinor took his offering and stared at Sennet. "I--um. Oh, this is strange. Are you...do you know what's going *on?*"

"Ceidrin sent me," Sennet said simply.

"Then...he's *alive?* Thank goodness." Elinor took a deep breath. "I--"

"Why don't you eat first, and then we'll talk?" Sennet suggested. "Edward and I have some things to discuss, as well."

"We do?" Edward asked, frowning, and followed her gaze to his mother's sword, half-hidden in an umbrella stand in the hallway.

Rose padded out from the kitchen, sunshine in her thoughts. The sun dimmed when she saw Sennet, and she glanced at Edward, as if waiting for him to tell her everything was okay.

"This is Sennet, Rose," Edward said. "She's a Healer."

Sennet crouched down and held out her hand. "Hi, Rose."

Elinor vanished into the kitchen with another troubled glance at Sennet, leaving them alone in the hallway. To prevent another line of questioning, Edward walked into the parlor and sat down.

Sennet followed him a moment later with Rose at her heels. "We do need to talk," she said. "Despite your wards, you are in danger here."

"I wouldn't be in danger here if everyone thought I was dead," Edward said, staring into the fire. When Rose bumped his hand with her nose, he remembered himself enough to stroke the soft fur on her head.

"Is that what you want?" Sennet asked. "To be forgotten? To live behind your wards until you die?"

"I was--" He wanted to say 'fine', but he hadn't been fine. He'd been starving to death, weary beyond belief, and ready to give up. He closed his eyes. "My mother petitioned someone in Faerie to intervene after I was cursed, but nothing ever came of it. I think she might have known who cursed me, but she never spoke that name to me."

"She kept you here," Sennet said, and he thought he heard a thread of pity in her voice. "Alone."

"What else was I to do?" Edward asked, his mind full of formless questions, old resentment, and even older anger. "I was a wolf. Nothing more. And when she died--"

"Do you know *how* she died?" Sennet asked.

Edward opened his eyes. "You're going to tell me she was murdered, aren't you?" He'd found her body, untouched, lying on a bed of ferns in the forest. It had taken him almost an entire day to bury her, and another two weeks to wait until he had hands to make a marker for her grave.

That was when he had closed off their land from prying eyes. That was when he'd retreated, at least until Arthur found a way past his wards.

"I don't know that for certain, but Lucien thinks so," Sennet said softly.

"She died while I was a wolf," Edward whispered. "She died, and I...I couldn't even say goodbye." He found tears on his cheeks, to his surprise, and surreptitiously wiped them away.

"The sword out in the hallway--it's in paintings at the castle," Sennet said. "Along with your mother."

"Your mother's in a painting at the castle?" Elinor asked, appearing in the doorway with a mug of--something--in her hand. She looked a bit better; more awake now, her skin not quite as pale. "Which castle?" She glanced between Edward and Sennet, no doubt feeling the tension in the room. "What's going on?"

Edward sighed. "My mother's name was Nidrea."

"Oh." Elinor sat her mug down on the table beside the bookcase. "I see." She stood there for a moment, and Edward let the silence fill him up until his ears rang with the absence of sound.

Rose *whuffed*. It didn't help.

"I'm sorry," he whispered, not turning around. "Perhaps I should have told you before, when you mentioned her name. But I didn't want to get involved. Not like this, at least."

"This is my fault," Elinor said, surprising him. "If I hadn't hit you, you wouldn't have *gotten* involved!"

"Until someone discovered his existence and decided to eliminate the competition," Sennet said. "He wouldn't have been uninvolved forever."

Edward shook his head and tried to smile. "I doubt it's entirely your fault, Elinor. Sennet's right. Someone would have found me eventually. But now that I am found--"

"At least *we* found you, and not my aunt," Elinor said. "But--"

"I think we've both agreed that there isn't any way Edward can assume the throne," Sennet said.

"I don't *want* to, regardless!" Edward stood up and stalked over to the bookcase. And then, when it gave him no peace, he turned, folded his arms, and glowered at them both. "My mother was not very fond of crowns. And neither am I."

"Will you come back with me to my house, at least?" Sennet asked. "To talk to Ceidrin? He won't bite. He'll understand."

"He'll understand what?" Elinor asked.

"That I cannot be king," Edward said. "That I want no part in this." He sighed. "Despite the fact that I seem to have no choice."

"You still have the option to close your wards and drive us all away," Sennet said. "But there is nothing in my house that will cause you any harm."

"I'm not sure I believe you," Edward said. He *wanted* to close off his house and land and vanish behind his wards. But if he did that; if he retreated and Elinor's aunt--his aunt, too, he realized--broke through his wards, he would have no one to turn to. He would have no allies.

And he was beginning to realize that he *needed* allies. Especially in this.

"I'll go with you," he said, and tried not to think about what going with them would entail. "Can Rose come, too?"

"Of course," Sennet said. "She is welcome to come."

"Just...just give me a little time," Edward whispered, and fled the room before she could insist on leaving right away. He heard Elinor call after him, but Sennet stopped her from following, her voice both calm and low.

And only Rose followed him, her presence a welcome silence at his back.

Despite the cold, he went outside and sat on the porch, shivering until he remembered he could shift shape and stay warm. But shifting shape seemed too much of a reminder as to what he would lose in a couple of days, so he sat and shivered with Rose pressed against his side. He didn't try to talk to her, and she stayed silent as well, her head on his knee, staring out at the snow.

When the first light of dawn cast long fingers of light across the snow, Edward stirred. Stiffly, he rose to his feet, realizing that he felt a bit--*lighter* now, as if the silence had strengthened him somehow. Leaving did not seem to be so terrifying a prospect now.

He walked inside with Rose beside him, liberated his mother's sword from the umbrella stand, and went in search of Sennet and Elinor.

He found them both in the kitchen, sharing a morning cup of tea. There was a third cup on the stove, waiting for him.

"Ceidrin's lover is a chef," Sennet said when he hesitated in the doorway. "I'm hoping I can convince him to cook us breakfast, if he's up to it."

Him? Edward decided not to ask. "I'm--ready when you are," he said instead.

"Will your wards let us leave?" Sennet asked.

"Yes."

"Then let's go," Sennet said. "Just take my hand, and hold onto Rose. You may want to close your eyes. It can be a bit disorienting."

Edward twined his fingers in Rose's fur and took Sennet's hand. She, in turn, grasped Elinor's hand and they stood there for a moment, entwined.

And then, almost before he could blink, they were--*somewhere else*. And for the first time in many years, he found himself curiously relaxed, as if nothing they could come up with could touch him now, even though he knew that wasn't true at all.

Chapter 18

Ceidrin had every intention of falling asleep and staying that way, but Sennet's doorbell rang an hour after she left and no one else seemed to be up to answer it.

Not quite predictably, there was an elf standing on her doorstep, a girl who looked vaguely familiar but whose name had never made it into Ceidrin's mind.

Sennet had not said what to do if anyone arrived asking for help. And as it was, the girl seemed fearful enough to leave if he left her standing out there, so he opened the door.

"Oh--you're alive!" She stepped back at the look on his face. "I...I told Sennet you hadn't gone home. She said she would find you--"

Sennet *had* mentioned some sort of warning, but Ceidrin had not been in the right frame of mind to comprehend what sort of warning she had received.

"Forgive me if my memory does not produce your name," Ceidrin said with as much gallantry as he could muster. "You know me, but do I know you?"

The girl hesitated. "My name is Dierin," she said. "I--"

He recognized her name, at least. "You are related to Lucien's side of the family."

"I am a servant in Oriellen's household," Dierin said softly. "Or I was. I will not be returning."

"Sennet is not here," Ceidrin said. "But if you swear to me that you intend no harm, I'll let you in to wait for her to return."

But Dierin was already backing away. "I'll come back later," she said. "But you may tell her I was here."

"Honestly, it wouldn't be any trouble," Ceidrin said. "There's hot water for tea on the stove, and I'm sure we could find you something to eat if you're hungry."

She hesitated.

"And if you plan to throw in your lot with us, you'd be safer here."

"And if I don't?" Dierin asked. "What if I want to be done with all of this?" She shook her head, her lips pressed together in a thin line. "They've resorted to kidnapping humans now, to get back at someone, I imagine--"

"Yes," Ceidrin said, and wondered if she spoke of Gene. "They kidnapped *my* human."

Dierin's hands flew to cover her lips. *"Yours?* But--they did not tell me whose he was. Oh, I'm sorry, Ceidrin; I can go back. I'll find him for you."

"He is already here," Ceidrin said. "And if I discover that you had anything to do with the torture he endured--"

"She gave me food and water," Gene said from the other side of the room. When Ceidrin glanced back at him, he smiled and shrugged. "I woke up and heard you talking--" He took a step away from the wall and swayed. "I'm sorry."

"You shouldn't be out of bed," Ceidrin said with a desperate glance at Dierin. "Come in. You can wait for Sennet here--"

"If I stay in bed, I'll just lie there and remember what they did to me," he whispered, and almost fell into Ceidrin's arms.

"What can I do to help you?" Ceidrin whispered in his ear.

Gene closed his eyes. "I need to be normal for a little while. Do you suppose Sennet would mind if I borrowed her kitchen?"

Ceidrin laughed. "I doubt very much she would care."

"Then I shall make you breakfast," Gene said, and smiled a genuine--if fragile--smile.

"If that makes you normal, then so be it," Ceidrin said. "I'll help."

Gene actually laughed at that, since he knew Ceidrin couldn't cook to save his life, but his laughter died when Dierin stepped through the door and closed it behind her.

"Perhaps I *shouldn't* stay," she whispered, obviously uncomfortable.

"Oh, no," Ceidrin said, deliberately misunderstanding her words. "There will be plenty for everyone, you included. Gene is rather incapable of cooking for two."

"But I--" She fell silent, then, as Ceidrin held out his hand to lead her to the kitchen.

"It's true," Gene said, some of his old laughter back in his voice. "It's a failing of mine, in truth."

As soon as Gene stepped into Sennet's kitchen, some bit of tension leaked out if his bearing. He stood for a moment, holding onto the countertop, then sighed. "There's a recipe I've been wanting to try--"

"Tell me what you need and I'll get it for you," Ceidrin said. He glanced at Dierin, who hovered in the doorway. "Sit down. Would you like a cup of tea?"

"I feel like I'm imposing," Dierin whispered, and Ceidrin thought he saw tears in her eyes.

"You aren't." Ceidrin said, but in truth, she was. Gene's point of anchor was the kitchen. Whenever they argued, he cooked, sometimes fantastical creations that Ceidrin had always managed to eat. He should have warned Sennet that Gene would need to cook. Ceidrin could only hope that Sennet's pantry would survive the onslaught. He smiled at Dierin. "Do you cook?"

"I can help," Dierin said. "I used to have a garden--"

"She can chop the vegetables, to spare your fingers," Gene said. "You can make pancakes. No one can mess up pancakes."

Ceidrin wasn't sure if he trusted Dierin with a knife, but he didn't want to shatter Gene's newfound calmness with a reminder of his captivity.

"I burn pancakes," he said, "but I'm willing to try."

Gene turned around. "Don't burn them this time," he said, almost begging.

Ceidrin glanced at Dierin, who was watching all of this with a stricken look on her face. He took a deep breath. If that was all Gene needed, then surely he could manage not to burn something *once*. It could be a fluke that would never happen again.

"I'll do my best," he said, which was as close to a promise as he could get.

Gene nodded. "Then I'll need flour, and eggs, and oil, and water--some green peppers, too. And mushrooms. Garlic, onions--a good knife--" He hesitated. "Sennet will be back soon. And she's bringing someone with her. Two someones. And a dog."

Ceidrin's heart leaped. Who had she *found?* "Then we'd best prepare," he said. "Dierin, are you okay with chopping the vegetables?"

"I'm fine," she said, clearly mystified by this turn of events. "How did...how do you *know?*"

Gene took a moment to reply. "The same way I knew Ceidrin would rescue me," he said softly, and opened the nearest drawer. He emerged with two knives in his hand, one of which he gave to Dierin, the other which he kept. "Eggs first, I think."

"Let's make breakfast," Ceidrin said, and opened Sennet's fridge.

Chapter 19

Elinor's only interaction with the network of Healers was from the stories everyone seemed to know about them. How they were neutral; completely neutral, and ageless, both women and men who could heal any manner of terrible wounds. They had become sort of mythological creatures in her mind, so to meet Sennet, who exuded normalcy, seemed somewhat anti-climactic.

And according to Sennet, anyone with a healing talent could be a Healer. There was no test; no apprenticeship per se; she could work with a more experienced Healer at first, but there was a shortage of Healers nowadays, and they needed all the help they could get.

This also made her fairly impervious to assassinations, since no one would dare harm a Healer for fear of having Healer support completely withdrawn forever.

That was not a failsafe, of course; Healers had been killed in the line of duty before. But it would help.

And Healers could not rule, so that would eliminate her name from the competition as well.

But all of that paled in comparison to the fact that Edward was Nidrea's son. He had seemed so--lost, almost, but that wasn't the word she wanted, really. He had spent the vast majority of his life cursed, and in a couple of days, he wouldn't be able to talk to anyone--except, perhaps, Rose, and he certainly could not rule a kingdom.

Not that he wanted to; he'd been quite adamant about that.

They appeared in Sennet's living room, a comfortably attired room that instantly pulled the tension from Elinor's bearing and put it *somewhere else*. Even Edward relaxed; his eyes were wide open, his lips curved up into a small smile.

"Not so bad, is it?" Sennet asked.

He hesitated, then shook his head. "No. Not so bad."

Elinor heard sounds coming from the direction of what had to be the kitchen; both voices and the clattering of pots and pans. Someone cursed--an elvish curse, but the crisis must not have been too terrible, because all she smelled was cooking food.

"It looks like we have a guest," Sennet murmured. "Would you mind waiting here for a minute? I'll be right back." She vanished through the doorway before they could reply.

"This isn't so bad, is it?" Elinor asked, sitting down in the nearest chair.

Edward opted to lean against the wall, his arms folded, his face both smooth and still. "Not so bad," he agreed, and smiled at Rose, who had made herself at home on the hearth rug. "But I can't help but feel a bit uneasy about all of this. I--"

Elinor heard Sennet's voice, but she couldn't understand what she was saying over the clattering. But a moment later, a blond elf Elinor recognized as Ceidrin walked out of the kitchen, wiping flour off his hands with a tattered towel. He nodded to Elinor, stared at Edward for a long moment, then briefly closed his eyes.

"I'm to tell you both that breakfast is ready if you're hungry," he said. "And if you have any hesitations to eat it, think of it as the last meal you'll ever eat that I helped with."

"That's a funny way to recommend your own cooking," Edward said after a moment of silence.

Ceidrin shuddered. "It is only because you don't know me that you say that," he said. "I can't cook. But--" He brandished his towel like a medal of honor. "I did *not* burn the pancakes."

"Who could burn something as simple as pancakes?" Elinor asked.

Ceidrin smiled. "You've no idea. Sennet informs me we'll all talk after breakfast, if that's okay with you." He said this as if he expected Edward to protest, but Edward only nodded, suddenly subdued and wary.

"That's fine," Elinor said.

"My name is Ceidrin," Ceidrin said to Edward. "I apologize for not introducing myself. Be welcome here, and eat with us."

"I would be pleased to eat with you," Edward said after a moment. "My name is Edward."

"You are Nidrea's son," Ceidrin said, seemingly unable to help himself.

"I thought you said we'd talk after breakfast," Elinor said, recognizing the hunted look on Edward's face.

"I...damn." Ceidrin's smile did not reach his eyes. "I *did* say that. I'm sorry. This is--"

"Awkward," Edward said with a slightly more genuine smile. "For what it's worth, yes. I am Nidrea's son."

"Unfortunately, it's worth much more than you probably realize," Ceidrin said. "But I promised to wait. So I will. We have omelets and pancakes and meat for those who eat it, and Gene opened a can of green beans for your dog. He said dogs love green beans." He sounded doubtful that was true, but Rose hopped up at the words and wagged her tail.

"Rose likes green beans," Edward said. "Evidently omelets as well." Rose barked. "As long as they don't have green peppers in them."

"You *communicate* with her?" Ceidrin asked, amazed.

Edward glanced at Elinor, and she thought she saw a glint of humor in his gaze. "It's not hard to do if you are a wolf for most of every month," he said.

Ceidrin spluttered a curse in Elvish, and probably would have said something he regretted if a dark haired human man had not appeared behind him.

"The food is getting cold," he said. "It's bad enough that Sennet took Dierin away, but I'd hate to waste all of this food." He nodded to Edward and smiled at Elinor. "I'm Gene. Sometimes Ceidrin's better half."

"More often than not," Ceidrin muttered, and shook his head. "Shall we eat?"

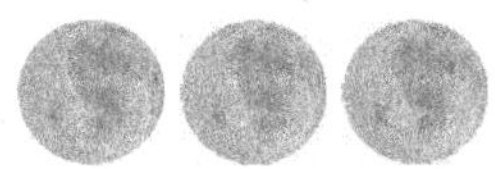

Sennet appeared halfway through the meal that Elinor couldn't eat--although the tea was superb--with a girl trailing behind her and a surprise--Lucien. Elinor hadn't seen Lucien for years, but he recognized her readily enough.

"I'm glad to see you here," he said, fixing himself a plate of food. "I tried to warn you, but they got to me first. Ceidrin saved my life."

"Sennet saved your life," Ceidrin said. "All I did was make it so she could."

"Either way, I wouldn't be here if it wasn't for you," Lucien said implacably. He nodded to Edward. "My name is Lucien."

"Edward," Edward said, and glanced at Sennet, who was busy explaining something to the elf--was this the 'Dierin' Gene had mentioned before?

When Lucien turned a questioning gaze to Ceidrin, who was probably biting his tongue, Elinor sighed.

"We can avoid this forever if we try hard enough," she said.

"Then why don't you have your talk over tea?" Gene suggested. "I'm fairly sure you--*we*--are all on the same side."

Ceidrin opened his mouth, as if to deny that Gene was involved at all, but closed it again without saying a word.

"This is Dierin," Sennet said a moment later. "Dierin, this is Edward and Elinor. You've met everyone else."

The girl smiled and nodded, but still looked terribly uncomfortable. Knowing the elves, it had something to do with class. Perhaps she was a poor cousin, or something like that. Elinor doubted anyone at the table would make her feel unwelcome, but the elves were *very* class-conscious, nonetheless.

"Edward and I don't know what has happened since--since my mother died," Elinor said. "Maybe we should start at the beginning?"

"The beginning starts with Nidrea," Ceidrin said with an apologetic glance at Edward. "But if you want to know what has happened since your mother died--" He spoke of the gathering, then, and what he had agreed to do. Of finding Lucien, of Dierin's warning to Sennet, and what had happened when the hounds arrived. Of his subsequent rescue, and then the rescue of Gene, who stared down at his plate through all of this, as if trying to ignore the summary of his pain.

Elinor spoke next, quietly, trying to make it through the telling without bursting into tears. She was an orphan now. And perhaps that made the thought of being a Healer a bit easier to bear. At least, with them, she'd belong to some sort of community. A surrogate family, of sorts.

Ceidrin asked no questions until she was finished. "I find it quite hard to believe that you just *happened* to--um--run over the very person everyone is now looking for," he said. "What possessed you to drive down that very road on that very evening?"

"I don't know," Elinor said, studiously not looking at Edward. "I wasn't thinking about finding anyone; much less Edward. I just wanted to get away from them. And I really didn't know who I could trust in Faerie, after that."

"Yes," Ceidrin said softly. "Imagine what would have happened if you'd confronted Oriellen?"

"Is *anyone* trustworthy?" Lucien asked. "Present company excepted, of course."

Ceidrin bit his lip. "I'd bet my life that Mahalia can be trusted," he said. "But as for the others--it's hard to say." He glanced at Edward, who had remained silent through all of this. Elinor had not mentioned his mother or his curse. Those two stories were Edward's alone to tell.

"I'm sorry," Dierin said softly. "But I don't understand where Edward falls in all of this. I--"

"My mother's name was Nidrea," Edward said, his voice equally soft.

Dierin scrambled up. "Oh...oh--"

It was quite obvious by the look on Edward's face that he did not understand her distress. Elinor tried to think of a tactful way to put it without resorting to the word 'commoner', but Ceidrin saved the day.

"Sit down," he said, his voice almost sharp. "Do you think we have the luxury here to resort to castle rankings? Is it not enough that you--by warning Sennet--saved my life? You are an honored guest here, Dierin."

She sat, awkwardly, and as far away from Edward as she could manage without being obvious about it. Elinor thought that everyone noticed anyway, but no one said a word.

"Castle *rankings*?" Edward asked, a certain amount of suspicion in his tone of voice.

"Surely you don't think that everyone can be royalty," Lucien said.

"Of course not," Edward replied. "But do your rankings go far enough to exclude kin from your table? I can see a family resemblance between both of you--"

"Dierin does belong to my branch of the family, yes," Lucien said. "But this is not something I introduced, or even like." He glanced at Ceidrin, as if daring him to interrupt. "You outrank us all anyway."

"Because I am Nidrea's son," Edward said shortly. "It doesn't matter that my father was human?"

"Not a bit," Ceidrin said. "Although some of the purists might protest, but let them protest."

"I can't be king," Edward said.

"That's what I hear," Ceidrin said, and Elinor wondered what he would say when Edward told them of his curse. "You also said something about--"

"A hundred years ago, I--*interrupted* someone's hunt," Edward said. "In anger at my meddling, the mistress of that hunt cursed me to be a wolf, save for a handful of days before and after the full moon."

"And you're still *sane*?" Lucien gasped.

"He wouldn't be sitting here if he wasn't still sane," Elinor said furiously.

"I've learned to live with what I am," Edward said, his voice still calm. "I have my mother's house and land. For most of the year I can easily feed myself." When no one responded, he continued, "My mother petitioned someone in Faerie to break the curse, and she might have known the name of the woman who cursed me. But she did not succeed before she died, and I have no record of her contact in Faerie."

"It was Oriellen, wasn't it?" Dierin whispered, her gaze fixed on her clenched hands. "She was the mistress of that hunt."

"She never gave me her name," Edward said. "And I've not seen her since."

"She was hunting a werewolf, wasn't she?" Dierin spoke in a monotone now, her eyes wet with unshed tears.

Edward glanced at Elinor, one eyebrow raised as if to ask if he should pursue this. "Yes, she was," he said. "Did you--*know* him?"

That had been a century ago, Elinor thought. Surely Dierin wasn't *that* old--

"My eldest brother," Dierin said. "I never knew him. His--*condition* was one of the reasons my parents were in disgrace. The court did not look kindly on werewolves back then." She kept her gaze on her hands. "I took the position in Oriellen's household in the hope of finding some sort of proof that she killed him."

"If the woman who cursed me was Oriellen, then she *did* kill him," Edward said. "In cold blood. Right in front of me."

"Would you recognize her if you saw her again?" Ceidrin asked.

Edward glanced at him and nodded. "Yes, unless she has changed her appearance in a century."

"Not that much," Dierin said, forgetting her wariness in the face of the truth. "Could I call Council to accuse her?"

"With only my word?" Edward asked.

"You could, but she would never admit it," Ceidrin said. "You need additional proof. If we could get one of her hounds alone, perhaps--do they all shift shape?"

"Yes," Dierin said, and shivered. "There are seven of them."

"I only saw five," Ceidrin said. "And that was enough. How did she create them?"

"I don't know," Dierin said. "But the one called Ahlos is the one you want to talk to. He's the eldest, and he *hates* her. She doesn't let him out much, though."

"I remember Ahlos," Gene said, frowning. "She had him on a leash. He was there when they--" He broke off with a stricken glance at Ceidrin. "He...he offered to kill me."

Ceidrin took a deep breath. "He *offered* to kill you?"

"If they got carried away," Gene said, and pushed his chair away from the table. "Are we finished eating?"

"You are *not* going to wash the dishes," Ceidrin said softly.

Gene shrugged. "Someone should," he said, and picked up his empty plate.

Ceidrin cast an anguished glance at Sennet, who shook her head, as if to tell him not to intervene.

Gene gathered up the dirty dishes, then carried them over to the sink in silence. Ceidrin watched him slowly start to fill the sink with soapy water, a lost and aching look on his face.

"He won't--"

"Give him time," Sennet murmured.

Ceidrin nodded unhappily, but his gaze never wavered from Gene.

"I saw five, too," Elinor said to break the silence. She couldn't help but remember how they had appeared out of nowhere and the strange way they shifted shape. "But if she keeps this Ahlos on a leash, how will we get to him?"

Sennet had, until now, listened quietly to the various stories, as if piecing the whole together in her head. "As I see it, you have two ways to find him. One--someone gets caught. That would get you into her castle. Or two, you make it so she has no choice *but* to release him."

"And how would we do *that?*" Edward asked, as if he suspected her answer would have something to do with him.

"Well--"

"No," Ceidrin said softly, still watching Gene. "I'm not giving *anyone* to Oriellen. And the alternative--unless we announce that Nidrea's son has been found, thus putting Edward in danger, we have no way to ensure she'll loose *all* her hounds."

"You rated five but I rate seven?" Edward asked.

"You're a bigger threat," Lucien said.

"Still, they couldn't get past your wards unless you let them inside," Elinor said.

"Could we set a trap?" Edward asked.

"For seven hounds?" Lucien stared at him. "How do you propose we do that? No one has successfully killed one of them--"

"If I had something that belonged to Ahlos--a scrap of clothing or a lock of hair or something like that--I could ensure that he was the *only* hound who could get beyond my wards."

"They can't get through?" Lucien asked. "At all?"

"*I* couldn't pierce them," Sennet said.

"You'd be under siege," Elinor said, not sure he realized the possible problems with that. "In the dead of winter. As a *wolf.*"

"We would still have to find something that belongs to Ahlos," Ceidrin said. He had finally looked away from Gene. "And that might prove a problem."

Dierin opened her mouth to speak, and suddenly, Elinor knew exactly what she would say.

"I could get it," Dierin said softly. She drew herself up when no one challenged her statement. "Oriellen doesn't know I've left for good. As far as she knows, I am visiting my elderly aunt."

"You do *have* an elderly aunt?" Elinor asked.

Dierin flushed. "Of course!"

"You would still be exposed," Ceidrin said to Edward. "We--I--will have to declare you found."

"I know," Edward said. "I have an idea about that, too. Could you pretend you've not spoken to me? I'm sure you'll be watched if you leave here; and you stole Oriellen's prisoner out from under her nose. She's not going to be happy with you."

"If I went to the castle seeking Ceidrin, and just happened to let it slip that I--um--hit you--" Elinor tried to think of a way such a plan would work.

"If Elinor had not taken you home--if you had been aware enough to fight her, what would you have done?" Sennet asked.

Edward hesitated, and Elinor knew he was trying on different answers for size. "I would have--"

"You would have vanished inside you wards, wounded or not," Elinor said, interrupting him. "And I wouldn't have been able to get through."

"You said you hit him, not that you almost *killed* him," Ceidrin said, and tried not to look too relieved when Gene wandered back over to the table. "How fast were you driving?"

From the doorway, Elinor saw Rose appear, her face inquisitive. She whined before Elinor could reply, and Edward jumped.

"She needs to go out," he said apologetically. "If you'll excuse me--"

"I'll take her," Gene offered. "If she'll come with me."

Edward glanced at Rose, then nodded. "She'll go with you."

As soon as Gene vanished down the hall with Rose at his side, Sennet held up her hands before Ceidrin could speak. "I can't tell you."

"I had no--" Ceidrin began, then sighed. "Perhaps I had every intention of asking you. I'm sorry."

"How long do you have before you're a--wolf?" Lucien asked.

"A day or two at most before I won't be able to shift back," Edward said. "Not long enough."

"Have you ever tried to break the curse?" Ceidrin asked, his voice low and worried.

Edward didn't justify that question with a reply. "We could sit here all day and still not come up with a plan," he said. "What are the odds that Oriellen will release Ahlos to hunt me? I don't think I rate *that* much of her attention. She doesn't know me, and if Elinor is convincing enough, she'll think that I'm dying, or wounded enough not to put up a fight."

"Will she send her hounds or come herself?" Elinor asked. "I'd think you would be a major threat to her plans--far beyond any of us."

"If she comes herself, can you keep her out?" Lucien asked. "If she's the one who cursed you?"

Edward opened his mouth to reply, then shook his head. "I am not certain of that," he said. "Even after a century, I don't know if she has any sort of hold over me."

"So any way we choose, we run into the possibility of failure," Ceidrin said. He closed his eyes and shook his head.

"What did you expect, that Oriellen would just leave you alone if you promised to behave?" Lucien half-rose from his chair. "Do you *want* her to be Queen? Or Meinren to be King?" He snorted laughter. "You've been too long from the court, Cousin."

"If I had my way, I would have been away much longer than this," Ceidrin snapped. "And all of--*them*--could rot in hell for all I care." *He* stood now, his face pale with anger, his hands clenched into fists.

"Ceidrin, wait," Sennet said, but he ignored her.

"I do not want the crown," Ceidrin growled.

"Then who shall have it, if not you?" Lucien asked. His voice was mild, but he watched Ceidrin closely, as if expecting him to attack.

Elinor found herself watching both of them, as a Healer, and feeling Ceidrin's grief and pain along with Lucien's frustration.

"We're all tired and frustrated," she said, trying to keep her voice calm, like Sennet's. "Perhaps we should reconvene in a few hours. A few hours won't make that much of a difference in anything at all. Dierin, how long do you think it would take for you to find something that belongs to Ahlos?"

"Maybe by tomorrow morning," Dierin said. "If Oriellen doesn't suspect me. I don't know if they've found out that your--" she glanced at Ceidrin. "If Gene is missing."

Edward glanced towards the kitchen door, as if expecting Gene to walk back into the room, but the doorway remained empty.

"Then go, and return as quickly as you can," Ceidrin said. "And then we'll decide what to do." He, too, glanced at the doorway, and frowned when Gene did not reappear.

"Be careful," Elinor said.

Dierin nodded. "I will."

As soon as she had left the house, Ceidrin pushed away from the table and stood. "Perhaps we *do* need some rest before we continue," he said, his voice rough. "Edward--it was nice to see you again." A smile flew across his face, then vanished under worry. "The last time I saw you, you were probably three years old."

"I don't remember," Edward said. "But I almost wish I did. My mother did not speak very often about her family."

"When this is over, if we all survive, I'll take you to meet some of the nicer Cousins," Ceidrin said, and hesitated. "I'll be in the...in our bedroom, for want of a better word, if...if Gene wants to know."

"I do have a library," Sennet said. "Other than that, my house doesn't lend much to entertainment. Make yourselves at home."

Lucien nodded and drifted away, looking troubled. Edward stood up a moment later.

"I think I'll just check on Rose," he said, and left Sennet and Elinor alone.

"Are you tired?" Sennet asked.

"No, not really," Elinor said. "I'm a little--worried, I guess. About what will happen."

"So am I," Sennet said, and smiled at her. "Would you like to meet another Healer? I'd like for at least one other person to know what's going on, just in case we need reinforcements."

We. Elinor shivered. "Can I really be one of you? A Healer, I mean?"

Sennet smiled. "You already are," she said. "Follow me."

Chapter 20

Ceidrin awoke when a hand--a *familiar* hand--softly brushed the hair away from his face. He opened his eyes and squinted at Gene, who smiled cautiously at him, his eyes full of something Ceidrin didn't want to define.

They had been together for almost forty years. And Ceidrin had thought--wrongly--that he knew every inch of the man he had taken as his soulmate.

"Hi," he said, and stretched, yawning. "How long have I been asleep?"

Gene shook his head. "Not long. Two hours, perhaps. Not much more."

Ceidrin levered himself up on one arm. "And you've been sitting there the whole time?" he asked. "The bed's big enough for both of us--"

"I know," Gene said. "I'm not tired. Perhaps I just wanted to watch you sleep."

This was the most Ceidrin had heard from him since his rescue, other than barking orders to his inexperienced helpers in the kitchen.

"Well--"

Gene interrupted him before he could continue. "They didn't do what you think they did," he whispered.

Ceidrin's breath froze in his throat. "They--"

Gene's lips quirked. "They wanted you to think the worst."

"I did," Ceidrin said. "Are you--" He wanted to ask Gene if he was certain, but why would he lie about something like that? "Still, they kidnapped you, and tortured you. I'm not inclined to forget that, or forgive."

"I wouldn't ask you to," Gene said. "But I want my own end to this." His eyes gleamed with sudden tears. "Don't shut me out."

Ceidrin hadn't thought at all about how to keep Gene safe, or whether it was his decision or Gene's to let him stay involved. "I--" He took a deep breath, quelling the urge to tell him that it was none of his business. It had become Gene's business when he'd moved into Ceidrin's house. "I had no intention of denying you an end to this," he said. *"But--you're not a wizard. They are."*

"You can give me protections against them," Gene said, his voice intense. "I know you can."

"You're right; I can," Ceidrin said. "And I will. But Gene--" He hadn't wanted to admit this in front of the rest of them; they seemed to think he was invulnerable. "I don't know if I'm strong enough to fight either of them. I survived one attack, but if Sennet hadn't come--" He closed his eyes and let himself fall back onto the bed. "If Sennet hadn't come, I'd be dead and so would you."

"What would happen to me if you assumed the throne?" Gene asked.

Ceidrin opened his eyes. "What? I have no intention--"

"Humor me," Gene said.

"If I--" Ceidrin didn't even want to *think* about it. "If I assumed the throne, which I am most certainly not going to do, then you would be my-- my consort."

Gene raised an eyebrow. "They'd let me stay?"

Ceidrin laughed. "Being king would have its advantages, and I *don't* think they'd let you leave after they tasted your cooking," he said. "They wouldn't have a choice, because if they forced you out, there would be Hell to pay."

"Then why--" Gene bit back his question. "You've never really talked to me about why you left Faerie," he said. "I know it wasn't only because of me. You had that house before I was ever in the picture."

"It's ancient history," Ceidrin said, and tried not to see the hurt in Gene's gaze.

"There was someone before me," Gene said lightly, as if he'd decided to weasel the story out of Ceidrin regardless of the circumstances.

"Yes. There was. He died." Ceidrin felt his lips curve into a smile as brittle as glass. "You do, you know. Eventually. Despite any effort to the contrary on my part."

"I know," Gene said.

"He died because we quarreled and I...I fled home with my tail between my legs like a beaten dog," Ceidrin said. "Only no one had ever bothered to tell me that if I stayed in Faerie for any space of time, the effects on my human lover would be disastrous. And I was gone--in Faerie--for a month. In the human world, thirty years had passed. And my--his name was Thomas, incidentally--Thomas was dead."

"I'm sorry," Gene said, perching himself on the edge of the bed. "I'm so sorry." He reached out his hand and wiped the tears from Ceidrin's cheeks. "I always wondered why you never stayed away for more than a week."

"Time isn't as different anymore," Ceidrin whispered. "Both our worlds have grown closer together. Eventually, they'll grow apart again, but for now, you're safe from that, at least." He blinked away the tears. "On her deathbed, my mother admitted that she had kept me in Faerie on purpose. She knew, you see. Thomas had tried to find me, and she kept him away." His lips twisted into a semblance of a smile. "She thought that might set me straight. She never approved of anything that I did."

"If you were king, you could change all of that," Gene said.

"But I don't *want* to be king," Ceidrin protested.

"I know," Gene said, his voice as soothing as his touch. "Just as Nidrea did not want to be Queen."

"It is not the same at all," Ceidrin snapped.

Gene sighed, as if he'd completely missed the point. "Show me how to protect myself. Just in case they try to take me again."

"How did they take you before?" Ceidrin asked, focusing on something he could understand.

Gene's lips twisted. "By surprise," he said. "I'd just gotten home from the grocery store when they appeared--"

Chapter 21

In hindsight, Edward realized he should have told someone that he needed some time alone to think. In hindsight, he would have found a way to go home, perhaps, and wander through the silence of the warded woods behind his house instead of the unknown forest around Sennet's little cottage. But it was broad daylight, and he neither sensed nor saw any sign that Sennet's house was being watched.

He had shifted shape early on, after finding Gene and Rose playing a frigid game of fetch in Sennet's backyard. At this time of the month, his wolf form was more familiar and more *concrete* than his human form anyway. If there were watchers, he saw no sign then, or when Gene had gone back inside and he had stepped outside of Sennet's wards to explore a new place.

Even Rose had not sensed a thing.

She followed him, of course, with only one longing thought of lying in front of Sennet's fireplace. For better or for worse, she considered Edward her Master now. He wasn't quite sure how he should feel about that. He wasn't quite sure of anything else, either; especially his wonderfully vague idea that could just as easily get everyone killed.

When the three hounds appeared--long and lean like greyhounds, save for the look in their eyes--he realized that Ceidrin's declaration that they had appeared out of nowhere was more than just simple inattention. They *appeared,* perhaps by magic, perhaps by deceit. Either way, he sensed nothing until they were far too close for comfort.

And they were not alone. A woman sat easily on a white elvish steed, too close in family resemblance to Ceidrin for any sort of comfort. And some part of Edward's human self recognized her.

"What is this?" she asked, just as Rose began to growl.

Sennet's house was in the human realm, or Edward *thought* it was, so the presence of an elf *here*--and the identity of that elf--could only mean one thing.

Oriellen suspected something. She might not know everything yet, but she knew enough to search out Sennet.

She dismounted, evidently assuming they would not run away--Edward had no doubt she would send her hounds to hunt him down if he tried--and stood beside her horse, muttering something under her breath. When she cast her spell--a net, of sorts that spiraled out in glittering arcs around both Edward and Rose, he had to struggle not to break it. If he did, she would know that he wasn't *just* a wolf.

And perhaps she knew already, because she frowned, glared at Rose, who had not stopped growling, and motioned to her hounds. "Kill them both."

Edward destroyed the net, shouted a silent order to Rose, and turned tail to run, dodging the hound who had circled behind them. Alone, he could probably outrun them, but Rose was only a dog. And mundane dogs could not outrun elvish hounds.

So he led two of them away from Sennet's house in the hope that Rose could get behind Sennet's wards before the third hound killed her--*if* Sennet's wards would hold--and find a way to warn the others. They would just have to worry about the crown without him, because he doubted the other hounds would give up until he was dead.

He managed to immobilize one with a hastily growled spell, but the other one gave him no respite. And despite the fact that Elinor had healed his wounds, she had not been able to heal his leg completely, and it was the first thing that threatened to collapse after he turned too quickly to avoid tumbling down a cliff.

And once the hound knew his weakness, it was only a matter of time before it acted on that knowledge.

Its teeth caught his hind leg--his *good* leg, not the leg that had been broken, and as Edward turned to snap at it, the hound went for his throat. In an instant, as they tumbled over each other in a flurry of snapping teeth and gouging claws, Edward knew he had to kill it or die trying.

He felt no joy when he tore out its throat, thus proving Lucien wrong that they couldn't be killed. But he had no time to rest on his laurels; another hound appeared out of nowhere--barreling into him before he could get to his feet--not the one that had followed Rose, thank goodness, but another one. Would she send all seven after him? Now that he had killed one, he thought, perhaps, that she would.

And Oriellen appeared to watch this part of the battle, her frown deepening when she saw the dead hound. Edward saw her move her hands in a complicated gesture--another spell, but he had no time to consider it until something cold as ice pierced his shoulder; until he remember Ceidrin's talk about the iron-loaded crossbow and saw the very same weapon in Oriellen's hands.

Edward collapsed, then, still fighting, bleeding from a dozen wounds, the snow that had remained throughout the battle bright red with both their blood. The hound was not much better off, but when *another* one appeared beside its mistress, Edward cast a net that fixed the first into place and wearily struggled to his feet to face the new foe.

"Who *are* you?" Oriellen asked, and flicked something at him with the tips of her fingers. Edward cast it aside.

His next spell, intended for the remaining hound, fell far short of its mark as she fired another bolt he barely dodged.

This time, the battle was far shorter than it had been before. This time, the hound went directly for his wounded leg--not the one already immobilized by the bolt, but the one Elinor had healed--and Edward heard the crack when it broke anew.

As a wolf, he could run on three legs, but not two. And he already knew that he did not want to shift shape in front of Oriellen.

"Hold," Oriellen said as the hound closed its teeth over Edward's throat.

Edward closed his eyes, gathered what small scraps of strength he could find, and prepared one last ditch attempt at escape.

"Open your eyes," Oriellen said, and a forgotten piece of Edward's mind wanted very desperately to obey her. He growled when she touched him--her hands were shockingly cold--and then she *did* something that cast all hope of freedom away. "Who *are* you?" she murmured, and something--something *broke* inside Edward's mind, shattered into pieces so sharp that they sliced everything they touched to shreds.

Edward screamed, and continued screaming, long after that last sane piece of his mind realized that she had torn something away from him; something so old and ingrained in his psyche that it shattered everything else with its passing.

He screamed until his voice gave out--his *human* voice; the wolf was gone now, dead, or worse--and curled up on the bloody ground, groping for some sort of stability--some sort of anchor--that would bring his mind back from destruction.

When she tried to tear something from his mind--his identity, perhaps--he fought her, but she found it anyway, and took that as easily as she had taken everything else.

And then, her touch receded. Alone and aching in every part of his mind and body, Edward opened his eyes and stared up at her.

Oriellen's face was a mixture of fury and shock. She stood above him with his blood on her hands and spun on her hound so quickly that Edward doubted it saw her move.

"He was supposed to be *dead!*"

The hound shifted shape at those words, its manner both cringing and wary.

"My lady--"

"Silence." She retreated into fury, the shock gone. Edward could only presume that she recognized him somehow, but did that mean she knew who he *was?*

He was having trouble breathing. He realized that with a sort of bemused detachment, almost as if he was watching himself from above. The pain had receded to a dull roar by now--at least, the pain from his *wounds* had receded, but his mind still felt flayed and raw. And he couldn't find enough strength to reach out to find something he could use to protect himself.

"How did you survive?" Oriellen asked the question expecting him to answer, but struggling against her was habit now, and not easily broken.

He felt something *snap* inside his mind; not quite as painful as the last time, but bad enough to almost send him careening into darkness.

But this wasn't Oriellen's doing; not this time. Whatever had broken, freed that last remaining piece of his mind that defined his *self,* and he used that--digging his fingers into the frozen dirt--to pull enough strength from the ground beneath him--from the stones and bedrock *under* him--to protect his mind from her touch.

He couldn't do much about his body, but his mind was his own again.

And faintly, very faintly on the very edge of his range of internal hearing, he felt Rose. Still alive. Safe.

Good girl.

"How did you *survive?*" Oriellen asked, and aimed the tiny crossbow at his heart. "Answer me!"

"My lady, he is dying," the hound whispered, and Edward heard some sort of echo in its voice; the faint whisper of the spell that kept it loyal to its mistress.

"He won't die," Oriellen snapped, but she hesitated before firing the crossbow into the ground right next to Edward's right ear.

He flinched, despite any effort to stay still.

"See? He's more awake than you think," Oriellen said, and fired the next bolt into Edward's other arm, effectively crippling him. "Go join your brother. Find out what else that damned Healer is hiding."

"And the wolf, my lady?"

Edward heard her reply through a fog of steadily encroaching darkness.

"The wolf? The wolf is coming with me."

Chapter 22

Sennet's first inclination that something was wrong was the furious barking outside. She wasn't the only one who noticed; Lucien appeared out of the library a moment after the cacophony started, and he followed her outside.

Rose stood at the very edge of the wards surrounding the garden, barking and growling at a hound--one of Oriellen's hounds, no doubt--that slunk into the trees as soon as Sennet and Lucien appeared.

"They've found us," Lucien said, his voice both soft and cold.

"Where's Edward?" Sennet asked, more concerned with his absence than the fact that the hound couldn't help but see Lucien.

Rose turned her head at Edward's name. The look in her eyes--Sennet's heart sank.

"Go back inside," she said to Lucien, who was too surprised at her tone of voice to protest.

As soon as he was gone, Sennet knelt down and held out her hand. "Rose, where is Edward?"

Whining, the black and white dog approached her hand, and just as Sennet stroked the soft fur on her head, she saw what Edward had done.

"Did he think he could fight them himself?" Sennet asked, and patted Rose on her head. "Thank you, Rose. Why don't we go and find him?"

If there was anything left to find.

Sennet heard the front door open behind her. "Go back inside," she said, not bothering to see who it was. "Stay inside, if you please, until I get back."

"But--" It was Elinor's voice, afraid and worried.

"Elinor, stay inside," Sennet said. "I don't want them to see you, too. They can't get through my wards, and they *won't* get through my wards while I am still alive."

"And if they kill you?" Lucien's voice cracked, as if he, too, realized what had probably happened. "Is Edward *dead?*"

"Rose doesn't know, and neither do I," Sennet said. "I intend to find out." Before they could ask any other questions, she stepped across her wards, and when she glanced back at the house, she saw that the front door was now shut.

Sennet stood completely still for a moment, straining her senses for any sign of Edward's pain. And his pain was not difficult to find. Even from this far away, she felt it, a vast engulfing agony that nearly swallowed her whole.

Rose whined. Sennet opened her eyes.

The hound stood about ten feet away, watching her, its eyes narrowed, its teeth bared.

"Even your mistress would not order the death of a Healer," Sennet said, hoping she was right. "Let us pass."

The hound shifted shape--not kindly, but in painful stages until it stood in front of her, seemingly of elvish origin. "My mistress bade me follow *her*--" it pointed to Rose, who growled, "and stop her from alerting you. I failed in my task."

Its shifting had only taken a handful of seconds, but seconds were important. Were they more vulnerable between shapes? Sennet made a mental note to mention that to Ceidrin when she returned.

"And her companion?" Sennet asked. "What of him?"

The hound cocked its head, as if it sensed her concern. "I don't know. Is he dead?"

"Not yet," Sennet said.

The hound frowned. "Pity. It might have been best if he died."

"Will you stop me from going to him?" Sennet asked.

"My mistress did not order me to," the hound said.

Sennet stared at it. "And you only do what your mistress wishes?"

The hound shrugged, shifted shape--quicker, this time, as if its body remembered its hound shape more fondly than its elvish one--and vanished into the trees.

"Stay near me," Sennet said, and twined her fingers through the fur around Rose's neck. It only took a moment to fix Edward's location in her mind--and recognize his tormentor--but by the time she found the spot, both Edward and Oriellen were gone.

Rose sniffed at a patch of bloody snow, and then the dead Hound. Sennet knelt at the edge of the worst of the blood and pulled an iron bolt out of the ground near where Edward had fallen. And then, with only the bolt in her hand and nothing more, she called Rose to her side again and returned home.

There were two hounds outside her wards when she arrived, but her house's front door was still closed and she saw nothing from the outside, looking in.

But everyone--Gene and Ceidrin, Elinor and Lucien--sat around the kitchen table, and Ceidrin was the first to speak when Sennet gently set the bolt down among them.

"Is he dead?"

"He wasn't," Sennet said. "But Oriellen took him before I could get there."

"She was there." Gene shivered. "With her hounds."

"Yes," Sennet said, watching Ceidrin's face. "She was there. Hunting in the human realm. I have *neighbors* here, you realize. We're not at all far from civilization."

"She is breaking the rules," Ceidrin said distantly, his eyes half-closed. "And now, at the least, she knows Lucien is here, and maybe me as well."

"Two of her hounds are outside," Sennet said. "No doubt wanting to get a glimpse of whomever else I am hiding."

"Why would they know of *your* presence?" Lucien asked.

Ceidrin touched the iron bolt, then snatched his hand away. "The last they know, I was with you," he said. "Can you--" He looked at Sennet now, his gaze full of torment. "Can you open another portal? Like we did for Gene?"

"Do you have a lock of Edward's hair?" Sennet asked. "There's blood, in the forest, and a dead hound, but blood doesn't work for portals unless you're very, very good. And my talents in that respect aren't good enough to use Edward's blood."

"There's a dead *hound?*" Lucien asked. "He *killed* one of them?" He sounded more surprised than joyous, as if he had half-believed his claim that they could not be killed.

"He killed one of them at a terrible price," Elinor reminded him. "Why did he leave your wards?"

"I don't think Edward's reasoning for stepping outside the wards are the issue here," Sennet said softly, still watching Ceidrin. He seemed poised on the brink of some terrible declaration, and she didn't have to guess what it would be. "How can we get him back?"

"By making sure Oriellen is distracted enough not to kill him," Ceidrin said quietly. "To give him a chance to escape."

"What kind of distraction are you planning?" Lucien asked suspiciously.

Ceidrin stood up. "I'm calling Council," he said. "This has gone far enough." He hesitated, and glanced down at Gene. "The only way anyone will accept my change of mind is if they think you died in Oriellen's dungeons, or soon after," he said. "Will you stay here? I swear I'll give you a chance at them once Edward is safe."

Gene stared at him for a moment, then nodded. "Of course."

"Gene's welcome to stay here," Sennet said. "But don't you need support to back your claim to the throne?"

"You have my support," Lucien said quietly.

Ceidrin nodded. "Thank you."

"And mine, of course," Elinor said. "If I can give it." She glanced at Sennet. "Can I?"

"A Healer's endorsement is a powerful thing," Sennet said. "But what will stop Oriellen from murdering Edward in retaliation?"

"Nothing," Ceidrin said. "But if I can get word to Dierin, if she is still free, then perhaps she can help. That's the only thing I can think of. I should have--"

"You couldn't have done anything differently," Gene said.

"And even Rose did not sense them coming," Sennet said. "They had no warning at all. And *I* didn't think they had found my house so quickly or I never would have let Edward and Rose go past my wards."

Ceidrin took a deep breath. "Our only potential problem with fictionalizing Gene's death is that Edward knows he's alive, and if Oriellen truthspells him--"

"Worry about that later," Sennet suggested. "She won't ask him until you show your hand and assume the throne. Gene and I will work on finding Dierin--she knows Gene is alive, too, for that matter."

"That means my life is in *your* hands, Elinor," Ceidrin said.

"Well, I can't be your food taster, but I'll do my best to keep you alive," Elinor replied. "I wish I could do something for Edward, though--"

"At the moment, the only thing we can do is hope he doesn't die before we can free him," Sennet said. "It's not enough, by any means, but it's the only thing we can do."

Chapter 23

Edward awoke the first time when someone tore both bolts from his arms in one swift movement that did not heighten the pain. He opened his eyes to dazzling brightness, closed them again, and heard a voice echo in his mind.

"He's awake."

It was a growling voice, as if the speaker had tusks instead of teeth. Or fangs.

When his unknown nursemaid tried to straighten his broken leg, he drifted away again with the growling voice ringing in his ears.

"You've lost him again."

"I know," a second voice snapped, and did something that brought him out of the darkness into cold clarity.

Edward reacted the only way he knew how, with the wards he'd placed around his mind. But the presence bending over him evaded his feeble defenses and left his mind alone. And a moment later, Edward felt half-familiar Healing magic course through his body, healing his wounds.

He spoke without opening his eyes. "If she will destroy your work by killing me, don't bother."

The owner of the growling voice laughed. "There's nothing wrong with his mind, at least. That--bodes better than the last one."

Edward felt a surge of guilt from the Healer, as if he had tried--and failed--to save whoever the last one had been. He opened his eyes and squinted up at the blinding light, realizing only after a moment that it was a lamp, bare of any shade, casting a light so bright that it chased away most of the shadows in the room.

"*She's* not the one I'm worried about," the Healer said, and motioned towards the lamp with one hand. The light dimmed enough for Edward to see, but the afterimages superimposed on his vision lasted for what seems like eons. "I apologize for the brightness. I can't see well in anything but full sunlight, and there's little of *that* down here."

"You're on your last light bulb," the growling voice said.

The Healer squinted down at Edward. "You'll have to find me more."

"And if I cannot?"

Edward couldn't see the owner of the voice any more than he could make out the features of the Healer's face. He squeezed his eyes shut, opened them, and tried again to focus.

"Then--" The Healer's hands lay lightly on Edward's left shoulder, his talent at work as he sat there, as if all he had to do was act as a conduit. "Then you'll have to be my guide dog."

For a moment, the growling voice did not reply. The Healer tensed, as if he realized he had gone too far with that comment, and opened his mouth, perhaps to refute his words.

"Do your work, boy," the voice finally whispered, sounding both weary and frustrated. "You won't go blind."

"Thank you," the Healer whispered, and bowed his head.

For the first time, Edward saw the Healer clearly. He stared, struggling to think why the boy looked so familiar.

"I'm Elinor's brother," the Healer said.

"As if that would mean anything to him, Luka," the growling voice snapped.

"It does," Edward whispered, and tried to sit up.

Luka gently pushed him back down. "Please. Lie still and let me work."

"How did you know?" Edward asked.

Luka shook his head. "Sometimes Healers can see--things," he whispered. "But I could recognize my sister's hand in the healing of your older wounds. She's--"

"She's alive," Edward said. "Or she was. I assume she's still safe."

"You were--with her?" Luka asked.

That was fairly simple news to uncover without betraying anyone else. "Yes."

Something moved past the lamp's burning light, a shadowy figure that seemed somehow wrong, as if one of the lumpish pieces should belong to a head that did not sit on mundane shoulders. Edward hadn't seen Oriellen's hounds shift shape, but the hunched figure reminded him of how they would look if they did, and perhaps, somehow, got caught between hound and human. Or elf.

"I hold no loyalty to anyone but the true king," Luka said.

"And who is that?" Edward asked, realizing that by right of birth, *he* was the true king, no matter how strange that sounded.

Luka glanced at the figure on the other side of the lamp.

It chuckled. "You'll find no argument here," it said. "She holds the key to my chains, but not my loyalty."

"By right of succession, that would be Ceidrin," Luka said. "He is--"

"I know Ceidrin," Edward whispered, and closed his eyes. "But what are *you* doing here?"

"Oriellen wouldn't allow Meinren to kill me," Luka said simply. "He killed my mother--" He said this last part as if hoping Edward would reply that his mother wasn't dead, but according to Ceidrin, she was. "He destroyed our home--"

"I thought the hounds killed your mother," Edward said. Ceidrin had *assumed* that, at least.

"No." Again, Luka glanced at the figure on the other side of the lamp. "Meinren killed her and left her body to burn in the sun."

"Elinor did not speak of a brother," Edward said before he could reconsider his words. Perhaps Elinor had a very good reason not to speak of her brother, despite his talk of loyalty to the true king.

"We--we don't speak," Luka said, and closed his eyes again. "She would be glad if I died, I'm sure." He turned away from Edward, then, and the figure behind the lamp spoke.

"Luka, *don't.*"

"Where is it?" Luka whispered, his voice cracking. "I can't--" His hands scrabbled across the dirty floor, searching for something Edward could not see. "Ahlos, *please.*"

Edward knew his wounds weren't completely healed, but he struggled to sit up anyway, trying to get a better glimpse of the figure in the shadows.

Ahlos was a hound; that much Edward already knew. But Edward's first impression had been correct--something had caught him between shapes, leaving him trapped in a twisted, ugly body with an iron ring around his neck. And perhaps it was the collar that kept him between shapes and not some spell.

Even then, twisted as he was, he moved quickly enough when Luka found what he was looking for, erupting from his corner with a curse as Luka turned around with a dagger in his hands.

Edward used up most of his strength to push himself away from both of them, his half-healed leg dragging uselessly across the ground.

Ahlos propelled Luka across the room and against the wall. The dagger fell from his hand and clattered on the floor; Edward thought about trying to crawl for it, but he doubted he would reach it in time to be able to protect himself.

And he didn't know what Luka had intended to do with the dagger, after all.

The Healer collapsed against Ahlos, his hands smeared with Edward's blood, his eyes squeezed closed, his teeth chattering. He did not speak or protest when Ahlos lowered him to the ground and turned towards Edward.

"When they brought him here, he was drugged almost out of his mind," he said, and moved with surprising grace to pick up the dagger. "I had hoped he could heal you before he lost himself again. When he's lucid--"

"I can *hear* you," Luka whispered.

Ahlos ignored him and handed the dagger to Edward, hilt first. "I am Ahlos." His voice had not improved, but had his appearance *altered* a bit while he stood there? "You've met Oriellen's hounds."

"I killed one of them," Edward said, and laid the dagger across his legs. "What would help him?" He thought he knew--both Luka and Elinor were half-vampires, after all, and perhaps blood was the only real cure for whatever drug they had given him.

"You *killed* one of them?" Ahlos whispered, and shook his head, just as Luka murmured something Edward didn't catch.

"Yes."

"And she let you live?" Ahlos seemed more surprised by that than the fact that he had managed to kill a hound.

"She--she recognized me," Edward said, and wondered how much he should tell them. A half-crazed Healer and a hound, even one such as Ahlos, seemed odd allies, if they could be called allies at all. "Are you bound to her?"

Ahlos laughed. "Of course I am bound to her. If I were not, she would be dead. As it stands, I am trapped like *this* and she remains alive."

"He...he means--" Luka's voice cracked. "He means--" He shuddered all over, and curled up into a ball on the floor, hiding his face in his hands.

"I know what he means," Ahlos said. "She could truthspell either of us--save, perhaps, for you--and force us to speak."

"A century ago, Oriellen cursed me with the form of a wolf, save for the night of the full moon," Edward said. "I was a wolf when she had her hounds attack."

"Yet you are not one now," Ahlos said. "Why not?"

"She forced me to shift shape," Edward said. He had not considered that she might have broken his curse, but he felt no inclination to shift shape now, even though he knew it was past the full moon.

"What is your name?" Luka asked. He had straightened up a bit, but his muscles still quivered, as if he was on the verge of a seizure. His eyes, once as brilliant as Elinor's, were glassy and dull, and a thin trickle of blood ran from a bitten lip.

"My name is Edward," Edward said. "What can I do to help you?"

Luka shook his head. "N...nothing. It w-will pass. I--" He stiffened, then, and his eyes rolled back in his head.

Ahlos barely managed to catch him before he fell. "You'll have to wait until he wakes up before he can finish healing you," he said. "Use the dagger if you need to."

"Isn't there a way to lure someone down here for him?" Edward asked. "Where *is* here, anyway?"

"You are in Faerie, in the cellars beneath Oriellen's dungeons," Ahlos said. "To lure someone down here would give away the fact that the dungeon's doors cannot be locked, and there is only one way out."

"Heavily guarded?" Edward asked, and drew a spiral in the dirt that covered the stone floor.

"Of course," Ahlos said.

"Are there others here?" Edward asked, remembering their conversation about the 'last one'.

"No." Ahlos didn't seem inclined to elaborate.

"If he stays down here, he will die," Edward said softly. "Wouldn't it be better to risk--"

"No," Ahlos growled, and touched the iron collar around his neck. "I cannot fight her. I cannot fight her will. This--*thing* around my neck ensures that I will be forced to obey whatever she demands. And she will demand his death."

"Despite the fact that he's a Healer?" Edward asked.

"He does not belong to the network of Healers," Ahlos said. "If she had known that before, I don't think she would have defended his life so vehemently."

Edward closed his eyes and leaned his head back against the wall. He wanted to sleep; to wake up and find that this was a terrible dream, but the throbbing pain from the ghost of his wounds and his leg would not let him rest. "And what if you manage to unlock--"

"Oriellen holds the only key," Ahlos snapped. "Do not tempt me with false hopes."

"Rose knows a spell to unlock locks," Edward whispered, his eyes still closed. Despite the pain; despite the fact that he knew he should stay awake, he felt himself drifting away.

"Who is Rose?" Ahlos asked.

With a tremendous effort, Edward opened his eyes. "A former wizard's dog," he said. "Her master taught her a spell."

"A *dog* learned a human spell?" Ahlos asked, his voice disbelieving.

"She's a very smart dog," Edward said. He shifted a bit in place, trying his best to sit up straighter so he wouldn't fall asleep.

"And do you know this spell?" Ahlos asked with ill-concealed impatience.

"She showed me," Edward said. "But I don't know if I have enough strength to cast it." He raised his arm and felt the new scar tissue and repaired muscle stretch. "Bend down."

Ahlos bent, his misshapen face emotionless; his eyes flat and cold. Edward touched the collar around his neck, felt the hatred that had placed it there, and pulled strength from the stones beneath him; the very bedrock of the castle itself. It was almost second nature to do so; he'd anchored his wards in stone, after all, and the rock in Faerie did not fight his touch.

In fact, it rumbled as he cast Rose's spell, and Edward felt a surge of something; some sort of energy, rise up out of the stone beneath him and spill across his connection with Ahlos.

The collar sprang open, and Ahlos stepped away, his form shifting as soon as he was free, until an elf stood there--with no sign of the creature he was--in front of Edward, both hands around his own throat as if to convince himself that the collar was truly gone.

He straightened up as Edward stared at him, his head swimming with unaccustomed power; his body as heavy as the stone beneath him, his vision darkening as the energy sought a place to stay.

He set it to work healing the rest of his wounds and felt it drain away, replaced by weariness so strong he felt himself falling sideways with no way to stop his descent.

Ahlos caught him and gently lowered him down to the ground. "I owe you my freedom," he murmured. "And I will bring him someone to drink."

Edward tried--and failed--to open his eyes. "She has no hold on you now?"

"None. I broke *that* spell years ago. Wait here. I'll be back." He vanished before Edward could stop him, and the silence was so thick and so complete that Edward did not fight the darkness when it carried him away.

Chapter 24

"But you *found* Nidrea's heir," Mahalia said for the second time, her voice still puzzled. "You found him and yet he cannot be king?"

"Yes," Ceidrin said, and hoped she didn't ask him to go into detail. "But that's not all. I wish to lodge a formal complaint against my aunt and cousin--Oriellen and Meinren--for murder, attempted murder, kidnapping, torture--"

"I've heard enough," Mahalia said, raising both her hands.

"And treachery," Ceidrin said. "And probably plotting against the crown. I have--"

"Proof?" Mahalia asked. "If I bring this to the Council, can you *prove* that they were involved in this?"

"I liberated Gene from Oriellen's dungeons," Ceidrin said softly. "They took him from the driveway of our *home* and tortured him, Aunt. Oriellen has hounds as well, who *attacked* Nidrea's son--"

"Is he *dead?*" Mahalia asked.

"We don't know," Ceidrin said. "I am hoping to pre-empt his death by doing this. I doubt that Oriellen knew who he was, but she took him away."

"We would have to summon both of them here to hear the charges against them," Mahalia said. "What else?"

"I thought you said you had heard enough," Ceidrin said. "Elinor's mother is dead, her house burned--"

"*Mmm*," Mahalia said. *"That* tragedy is being blamed on Elinor's brother."

"By whom?" Ceidrin asked. "Elinor saw the hounds. They chased her into the human realm. Oriellen snatched *Edward* in the human realm--"

"By Oriellen and Meinren, of course," Mahalia said, and rose from her desk to pace the room. "Is Elinor still outside?"

"I hope so," Ceidrin said. "She's my bodyguard."

Mahalia stared at him for a moment, unsmiling. "You expect them to attack you *here*?"

"Once they find out what I've done, I expect no less from them," Ceidrin said. "They managed to murder Isobel, and probably Nidrea as well--"

"Elinor's brother was Isobel's confidant, and the last person to see her alive," Mahalia said. "We've been looking for him since she died. Did no one tell you? Are you certain you have the right villain?"

"No one told me anything, save that she was dead," Ceidrin said, and closed his eyes. "Is her brother also a Healer?"

"Yes. He is." Mahalia stopped in front of a floor-to-ceiling mirror and regarded her reflection for a moment, then frowned, as if she had seen some minute imperfection. "Call Elinor, please."

Ceidrin opened the door and stuck his head out into the hall. The hallway was deserted; an odd thing, in truth, since this part of the castle was well-traveled and often used. At his request, Mahalia had set wards around the room, but she had called him paranoid. And now, Ceidrin wondered if he should have insisted that Elinor join him in the first place.

"She's not--" He turned back to face Mahalia, just in time to see her crumple where she stood, her eyes wide and fading, her hands clutching at the dull iron bolt that jutted from her chest.

For a second he stood frozen, his mind refusing to accept what his eyes already knew. But even in that second, some piece of his subconscious registered a threat, and when he turned around, two of the bolts hung quivering in the air behind him, caught in the net of a ward he didn't recall casting.

And it was Meinren behind him, not Oriellen, holding one of those damned crossbows, his eyes narrowed, his lips thinned.

Elinor--Elinor lay bound behind him with blood in her hair, her eyes closed, but breathing.

"They are *iron*," Meinren said, as if that one word would crumble Ceidrin's ward at its utterance.

"I suppose, then, it is an advantage to live with a human chef who insists on cooking with the very same metal," Ceidrin said, his voice very calm. "Will they kill *you?* I've already survived them once."

He realized, then, that his calmness belied an anger so terrible that he almost could not hear over its fury. Meinren saw the truth in his gaze, and stepped back.

Ceidrin plucked the bolts from the air and threw them on the ground. "This--" He motioned behind him where Mahalia lay. "This is *treason,* you realize. Punishable by death."

Meinren's lip curled. "It would only be treason if you were king," he said stiffly. "You had one warning--" His finger tightened on the crossbow's trigger.

Absolutely unable to help himself, Ceidrin sketched him a mocking bow. "Treason."

"No." Meinren shook his head. "No. You swore--"

"Yes, I did," Ceidrin said, and saw Elinor's eyes slide open. "I swore. I wanted nothing to do with the crown or its kingdom, but you made one fatal mistake, Cousin. Perhaps more than one, in truth."

"The only mistake I made is telling my mother's hounds not to kill you," Meinren spat. He fired another bolt; Ceidrin deflected it without a passing thought.

"No. You kidnapped an *innocent*," he said, his voice full of a terrible power that seemed to emanate from the stones beneath his feet. "You kidnapped and *tortured* the man I love."

"A human." Meinren dismissed Gene with a toss of his head. "They are so fragile. So easily hurt."

"Yes, they are," Ceidrin said. "And it's a shame *we're* not more easily killed." Using the power that surrounded him, he broke Elinor's bonds and shattered the spell Meinren had cast across the hallway. Elinor sat up, holding her head, her eyes squeezed shut, her mouth pinched. "Elinor, can you see to Aunt Mahalia? I'm afraid--"

"No need," Mahalia's dry voice came from behind, ringed with pain, but also buoyed by fury. "There are advantages to wearing so much jewelry, but my necklace might never be the same again." She motioned towards Meinren, and the crossbow fell from his hands. "I'd add attempted murder to your charge of treason, Ceidrin."

"Attempted murder, murder, treason, kidnapping--"

"My *mother*--" Meinren began.

"Your mother is not here," Elinor said, her voice cold. "I am a member of the Healer network now--did you bother to *think* before you wounded a Healer in the line of duty?"

"He doesn't think," Ceidrin said as Meinren's face paled. "He never has."

There were more elves in the hallway now, all staring, all hesitating, as if they did not quite know what to do.

"I call Council," Ceidrin said, almost relieved that he did not have to continue the fiction of Gene's death. "And I will submit three witnesses in addition to myself and Elinor: Lucien, Sennet, and Gene. I will also demand the release of the hound called Ahlos, Elinor's brother, and Edward Lange. And anyone else you or your mother might be hiding in your dungeons."

"A *human?*" Meinren made an abortive move to escape, but Ceidrin's net settled over his skin, pulling him backwards until he sank into the wall itself. "Your damned brother is the murderer--"

"My brother may be a bit unstable, but I can't see him murdering anyone," Elinor said sharply.

"Do I have to gag you?" Ceidrin asked. "You're only making it worse for yourself. I call Dierin as witness as well--"

Meinren laughed before he could stop himself, then shut up when Ceidrin swung around to face him.

"Speak," he demanded.

"Dierin is dead," Meinren said. "She was a traitor, and she died like a traitor--"

"Would someone find out if that is true?" Ceidrin asked quietly, and used a bit of the power to gag Meinren before he damned himself any further--or talked himself into an early grave.

"Of course," the nearest elf said, still wary, but willing to help. "I know her family; I'll check."

Ceidrin had never seen him before, but Mahalia whispered the name 'Rhys' in his ear.

"He is trustworthy," she murmured. "Distantly related to Elinor's side of the family."

"Thank you," Ceidrin said to him. "If anyone tries to stop you from letting me know what you've found--"

"They will not," Mahalia said, and swept out of the room, dropping the remarkably unbloodied iron bolt at Meinren's feet. "Ceidrin has called Council," she said, and the declaration reverberated through the castle.

"Give me an hour to prepare," Ceidrin said. "To gather my witnesses."

"Granted," Mahalia said. "You *are* our king, after all."

Ceidrin tried not to flinch when he heard that small tidbit of news pass between the gathered elves like a wildfire, and continue its spread through the castle. He wasn't quite sure how he knew that; he'd never found the castle particularly responsive at all.

"I've heard it wears off in time," Elinor whispered as two elves approached to take Meinren away.

"What?" Ceidrin asked, watching them try to figure out how to pry him from the wall.

"You can sense everything, can't you?" Elinor smiled. "The one time I met Aunt Isobel--she told me to call her that--she said she knew what was happening in any given part of the castle at any given time."

"She told you that?"

"She said that was part of being Queen," Elinor said. "I was eight years old, and very impressed."

"She was a good Queen," Ceidrin said, and took pity on the elves. "Why don't you just leave him there?"

"In the wall?" one elf asked. "But--"

"It's secure," Ceidrin said. "I'll bring him to the Council meeting myself. If it makes you feel any better, you can guard him."

Meinren made a furious set of noises behind the gag. Ceidrin smiled brightly at him, and he subsided.

"At the moment, I believe we're in need of a mirror," Elinor said.

"We'll use this one," Ceidrin said, and retreated into Mahalia's meeting room, firmly closing the door behind him.

He leaned on it for a long moment, his mind replaying the last few minutes and trying to come up with a good explanation as to why he was not dead.

"Are you okay?" Elinor asked.

Ceidrin opened his eyes. "It's nothing you can fix," he said. "I--I didn't expect it to happen like this." He stared at the spot where Mahalia had fallen. Had her necklace *truly* blocked the bolt from killing her?

"It never does," Elinor said, and for a moment, Ceidrin thought she would add something else to that proclamation. "What does my brother have to do with this? He was part of Meinren's group of 'friends' once; we haven't spoken since my father died." She stared into the mirror, frowning. "I didn't know he was here."

Ceidrin had no lock of hair to find Edward, but he knew the general location of Oriellen's castle. "Mahalia said that he is suspected of killing your mother, and that he was the last person--save for the murderer--to see Isobel alive. He's wanted for questioning, but they seem to assume he ran away."

"I thought we were going to tell Sennet--" Elinor said as a perfectly normal looking stone castle appeared in the mirror like a postcard from Faerie.

"That's your assignment," Ceidrin said. "I'm going after Edward."

"By yourself. With no Healer to save you if Oriellen tries to kill you." Elinor shook her head. "No way. We contact Sennet and the others first, bring them here, and then we *all* can go with you to find Edward."

"If I die, Lucien is first in line to take the throne," Ceidrin said, and opened the portal. "Don't you think it would be prudent for me to leave him behind? And if you contact Sennet now, he'll insist on coming."

"I'm coming after you, then," Elinor said. "I'll be *right* behind you."

"That's fine," Ceidrin said, watching the castle for any sign of life. He couldn't even see any guards on the battlements. "Tell Gene not to kill

Meinren." Before she could answer, he stepped through and closed the portal behind him.

Even here, he felt a strange sort of power from the stones under his feet. It was almost as if the kingdom itself recognized him, and he wondered if that were true. Was this pre-ordained? Had he been fooled all along into believing that he actually had a choice?

Preternaturally aware of everything around him, Ceidrin set his sights on the castle and walked up to the nearest door.

It opened at his touch. Frowning, he slipped inside.

Chapter 25

When Edward opened his eyes, he saw Ahlos first, bending over Luka's sprawled out body with a cup in one hand and a half-empty glass pitcher beside him. The body of an elf--presumably the source of the blood in the pitcher--lay against the far wall, but Ahlos had not escaped unscathed. He'd tied a makeshift bandage around his arm, but the shredded sleeve of his shirt was wet with blood.

"He fought," Ahlos said as soon as he realized Edward was awake. "The others did not."

"Others?" Edward asked, struggling to sit up. "How many--"

"Five." Ahlos' grin held nothing but a mad sense of joy. "I did *not* go in search of Oriellen. Yet."

"You killed five of her guards and you don't expect anyone to notice?" Edward asked.

Ahlos shook his head. "They aren't dead. They're locked in another room, bound, gagged, and warded. I didn't know how much blood he would need." He grinned again. "And anyway, Oriellen will have worse things to worry about. The kingdom has chosen its king."

"The *kingdom* has chosen--?"

"You should feel a bit of it," Ahlos said. "You healed yourself with some of that very same power."

"And you feel it too?" Edward asked, inordinately relieved that the kingdom hadn't chosen *him*.

Ahlos hesitated. "If I say yes, you'll think I'm something I'm not," he whispered. "If I say no, you'll wonder where I got my information."

Edward slowly bent his once-broken leg and used the wall as a crutch to help him stand. It held, with only a passing ache when he put his full weight on it. Wherever the power had come from; the kingdom or the stones under his feet, it had healed the rest of his wounds.

"Then I won't insist you answer," he said. "Do you know what kind of drug they gave him?"

Ahlos glanced down at Luka. "From what he has said, it was something Meinren came up with to combat his vision problem," he said. "Only, it didn't quite work the way they planned it to work. And they deliberately gave him an overdose before he came here."

"Or perhaps it worked just fine," Edward said. "He makes a good scapegoat if he's known to be a bit--"

"Unstable?" Ahlos' eyes narrowed. "That's true." He glanced back at the elf, as if gauging how much blood he had left in his veins, then pressed his cup to Luka's lips. "He has never been very--observant."

"But he's a Healer," Edward said. "That has to count for something." He walked across the room without limping once. "How long are you planning to stay here?"

"How long will it take for Oriellen to realize something is wrong?" Ahlos asked. "If you take him out of here--"

"I've never been here before," Edward said. "I have no idea where to go or how to find Elinor and the others."

Ahlos stood. "I can't let her get away," he whispered. "You couldn't *begin* to understand. Take him out of here. Please."

"I understand that she cursed me a century ago, and I've spent the last hundred years only human during the space of a couple of days a month," Edward said quietly. He felt something surge in the power around them now--a welcoming, of sorts, as if someone new had just walked through the front door. "You don't have to do this alone. She owes me something, too."

Ahlos cocked his head, his eyes half-closed, listening to the same thing. "Ceidrin is here."

"By himself?" Edward asked, wondering how he had managed that feat, since he was--no doubt--now king.

"I took the guards at the gate, and opened a few doors," Ahlos said. "I thought someone might come for you."

"And Oriellen?" Edward asked. "Where is she?"

Ahlos bared his teeth. "Summoning her hounds," he said. "I must go."

Edward dropped to his knees beside Luka, and carefully pulled him up. His eyes half-opened, but they were glazed and unaware; despite the blood he had drunk, he was still lost in the throes of the drug.

"I must go," Ahlos repeated.

"Then go," Edward said. "I'm not leaving him here." He tucked the dagger into a pocket of his ruined coat and stood up with Luka's arm across his shoulders. It was an awkward position, made even worse by Luka's dead weight.

Ahlos draped his other arm across his own shoulders a moment later. "We will--move quicker if we work together," he said. "I'll show you the way out."

Carefully, still slowly, they moved down the hall and to the door that led to freedom.

Chapter 26

"What are *you* doing here?"

Ceidrin had half-expected to be stopped much sooner as he ventured through the silent castle, but he had not found a single soul, until now.

Oriellen stood in the hallway behind him with four hounds at her side, their beauty belying the fact that she had used them for ill.

"The door was open," Ceidrin said, which was the truth. "I saw no guards; no sign of life. I was concerned, Aunt."

Her lip started to curl, but then she thought better of it and smiled instead. "My guards must be--" For a moment, she couldn't think of a word to say. "Detained, I suppose. I can't *imagine* how the door became unlocked."

"You should keep better track of your guards," Ceidrin said. "But in truth, I came to speak to you, Aunt, and invite you back to the castle to answer the charges against you."

"Charges? Brought by whom?"

Ceidrin smiled, although he knew that would probably make it worse, at least in *her* mind. "Brought by me." He hesitated. "Meinren is already in custody, after attempting to kill our Aunt Mahalia. You have a lot to answer for, Aunt."

"I have no control over my son's actions," Oriellen snapped, and her hounds began to growl.

"Would you stoop so low as to kill your king?" Ceidrin asked softly. "It would only be worse for you if I die. Too many people know what you have done." When she did not reply, he continued, his voice mild. "I came for Edward, Elinor's brother Luka, and the hound called Ahlos, as well. Dierin's death is on *your* conscience, and you will be punished for it."

"If you die here, who will stop me from taking your crown?" Oriellen asked, her voice harsh. "No one!"

"I will stop you," a voice said from behind Ceidrin. He glanced back, not turning his back on Oriellen or her hounds, and saw Edward and an elf appear from around a corner with a boy--obviously Elinor's brother-- unconscious between them. The elf left Edward to support Luka's weight and nodded to Ceidrin.

"I will stop you," he said again.

Oriellen's face underwent a very interesting change as the elf advanced past Ceidrin and closed in the distance between them. He had never seen her actually *afraid* of anything; she'd always treated the world as an irritation, not something to fear. But this elf awoke something inside of her that stripped her of all sense and left her with fury as her only recourse.

She sent the hounds to kill him, but the elf seemed to expect this. He shifted shape in one fluid moment, almost as if he'd been practicing, and tore into them, *his* fury no match for their might.

Over the sound of snapping teeth and growling hounds, Ceidrin met Oriellen's gaze. When the last hound fell, he heard Edward curse behind him, and without looking to see where he was, reached out to stop him from joining the fray.

"He took the dagger," Edward said as the hound--who had to be Ahlos--shifted shape again.

Ceidrin turned his back on both his Aunt and her former hound as the dagger flashed. He did not have to watch her die.

"Elinor's brother--is he wounded?" He could concentrate on that instead of wondering if he should have tried to stop Ahlos' revenge and keep Oriellen alive for some sort of sentencing.

"He--they gave him an overdose of some sort of drug," Edward said. "I'm not sure how sane he will be when he wakes up."

"He will have the best of care until he is well," Ceidrin said softly. "Elinor and the others will probably be here soon."

"And what would you like me to do with the prisoner?" Ahlos asked, appearing beside him with the dagger in his hand. He handed it back to Edward, hilt-first, then nodded back to the carnage. "I thought I wanted to kill her. But I think I would rather have the story told in full."

Ceidrin stared at him. "I was willing to give you her death," he said. "I could have tried to stop you."

"I know." Ahlos hesitated. "But there has been enough death, I think. I would rather see them punished."

"Your name is Ahlos," Ceidrin said.

"It--" Ahlos glanced at Edward, and almost smiled. "It didn't used to be. A long time ago, my name was Jeremin. I am Oriellen's brother." He let out his breath, then, one hand pressing against his stomach where Ceidrin could see fresh blood. "My sister found me dying and nursed me back to health. And then she bound my will and my--"

Ceidrin caught his arm as he staggered sideways, his face suddenly grey. "You'll have time to tell your story," he said. "All the time you need." Gently, he lowered Ahlos down to the ground. "Edward, would you mind checking to see if our cavalry has arrived? They may not know we're here--"

Almost before he finished speaking, Sennet appeared in the hallway, with Lucien, Gene, and Elinor close behind. Behind *them* were elves--a whole troop of soldiers who seemed quite relieved that he was still standing and not lying dead like the hounds or wounded like almost everyone else.

"Oriellen is to be taken back to the castle to answer the charges against her," he said before anyone could speak. "Sennet--there are wounded here--"

"I see that," Sennet said mildly as the elves rushed to obey his orders. "I'm glad to see you whole. I wasn't quite sure what we'd find here, so I brought some reinforcements."

"Thank you," Ceidrin said, his gaze on Gene, who seemed more angry than relieved. "Lucien, will you go back to the castle and explain to Mahalia what happened here?"

"I'm not sure I *know* what happened here," Lucien said, staring at the dead hounds. "Who is this?" He indicated Ahlos, frowning. "He looks familiar."

"All will be revealed," Ceidrin said. "In due time."

He left Elinor and Sennet to do what they did best, and walked past Edward to where Gene stood against the wall.

"You saved my life," he said as soon as he was close enough to speak without shouting.

The retort on Gene's lips melted away. "What? How could I save your life if I wasn't anywhere *near* here?" He had more to say--*much more*, knowing Gene--but Ceidrin placed one finger against his lips to silence him.

"You saved my life," he repeated. "However much I hate to admit it, I suppose cast iron *does* have its advantages."

It was a long-standing and very silly argument that Ceidrin had never once let him win--until now.

Gene grinned. "So I was right, then," he said, his anger--at least temporarily--forgotten.

Ceidrin rolled his eyes. "Yes. You were right."

Chapter 27

Given the elves' love of stories, the entire sordid tale took almost two weeks to tell. Once the dam was broken, the secrets Meinren and Oriellen had kept hidden overflowed into many facets of the court itself, and they weren't the only ones punished for their involvement.

They *were* the only ones sentenced to death.

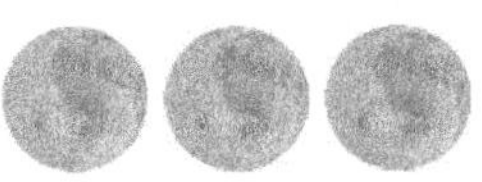

Later, after the tale was told, Sennet gifted Edward the use of a portal, and he slipped away with Rose, confident that no one would notice his absence. Ceidrin had a kingdom to run; Elinor had her brother to look after. Gene had decided to make the best of a difficult decision, and had overthrown the castle kitchen, much to the dismay of the cooks. Even Ahlos had been reinstated into his former life; while Ceidrin could not give him back the time he had lost, he made up for it by giving him a seat on the Council and a place to live.

Back home, Edward found the promise of spring in a carpet of early crocuses that pushed through the melting snow, their brightly colored flowers a wonderful harbinger of what was to come. Finding food to eat wasn't difficult once he remembered how to set traps, and there was plenty of greenery to forage from, including a few bulbs of wild garlic he found in the remnants of the garden.

Rose proved to be an adequate hunter herself, but sometimes, Edward found himself envying her as she stalked through the budding saplings in search of her supper.

He had not tried to shift shape since Oriellen had broken her curse.

A few weeks after he returned to the house, he awoke to find moonlight streaming in his bedroom window and Rose standing with her nose pressed against the glass, watching the moonlit forest outside. Edward joined her at the window, staring down at their stark and beautiful surroundings, and felt something half-familiar stir in his mind.

Not the curse, but the echo of *what once was*--the echo of a wolf.

Almost in a dream, he followed Rose down the stairs, and opened the front door. Barefoot, he stopped on the edge of the porch and shivered as a cold breeze--the last breath of winter?--blew across his face.

Rose whined, glancing up at him, her tail wagging. *Want to run.*

It had taken him only a week to teach her words instead of pictures.

"Me, too," Edward said, and sat on the steps beside her. "But I--I don't know if it will work." And what if shifting shape--if he still *could*--triggered the curse again? Was it broken forever?

Would it be so terrible if it were not?

He closed his eyes and felt tears slip down his cheeks. He had not allowed himself to grieve for his wolf form; that had seemed almost silly, grieving for a curse. But it had been a part of himself for so long that he felt a bit lost without it.

When he opened his eyes, he saw the world through the eyes of a wolf.

For a moment, Edward just sat there, stunned and confused, until Rose barked and bounded down the steps. Despite what his mind thought, his body knew what to do, and he joined her, glorying as they chased each other through the melting snow; actually having *fun* as he explored the edges of his land on four legs instead of two.

When they returned to the house, he saw Elinor sitting on the porch, waiting for him.

She stood up as they approached, and almost dropped the basket she carried. "Oh--"

Edward shifted shape before she could finish her sentence. "It's okay," he said. "The curse is still broken."

"But you're still a wolf," Elinor said. "I don't understand."

"I *chose* this," Edward said, and knew that to be true. "There are certain-- advantages I'm not willing to give up." He smiled at her, and after a moment, she smiled back. "What brings you here?"

"I wasn't sure your wards would let me inside," Elinor said. "And I'm sorry I didn't try to visit until now. Gene sent me with a basket of food, and Ceidrin said you can't stay away forever."

"I thought it was time to go home," Edward said. "But I don't intend to stay away forever. How is your brother?"

He hadn't really considered going back, but Elinor didn't need to know that.

"He--he woke up yesterday," Elinor said. "And he talked. He talked quite a bit, actually. Meinren killed Isobel with the same drug he gave Luka. My brother tried to stop him, and--" She shrugged. "That's how he came to be in Oriellen's dungeons."

"And will he recover?" Edward asked.

"It will take time," Elinor replied. "And I didn't come here to talk about my brother, Edward. I--" She frowned. "You're barefoot."

"It seems to be a failing of mine; finding shoes," Edward said. "Would you like to come inside?"

"I wondered if I could help with that," Elinor said, ignoring his question. "I've decided to sell my father's house, you see, and my mother wasn't badly off, either--and you'll need some help getting used to the modern world."

Despite the fact that *Elinor* was the one offering the help, Edward felt that old distrust raise its head again. "And you're offering me this in exchange for what?" he asked.

Elinor bit her lip. "Sennet said that I need some help with wards," she said. "She said that I have the talent, but not the training. I thought--if you agreed, of course--that you might be able to--to teach me?"

"Well." Edward touched the porch railing and felt the wards that kept the world from invading his home pulse through it. "I suppose--I suppose we could teach each other. And my house *could* use a new roof."

Elinor grinned. "And you won't stay away from Faerie? Ceidrin said you're always welcome."

That was a bit more difficult, but why *should* he shut everyone out? "I won't stay away forever," he said. "Maybe--maybe Rose and I will come back with you for a little while. I have something I want to give to Ceidrin."

That something was his mother's sword, long unused and almost forgotten. It deserved to return to its original home, in the place where it had been given to a princess who had then cast it and everything it stood for aside.

Edward could not fault his mother for abandoning her duties for the love of his father. But he'd wondered-- especially now--if she had ever wished that things had turned out differently.

"Would you like to come inside?" he asked again.

"I would love to come inside," Elinor said, and followed him through the door.

You can find ALL our books up on our website at:

http://www.writers-exchange.com

All Jennifer's books:

http://www.writers-exchange.com/Jennifer-St-Clair/

all our fantasy novels:

http://www.writers-exchange.com/category/genres/fantasy/

About the Author

Jennifer St. Clair grew up in Southern Ohio and spent most of her childhood in the woods around her home. She wrote her first novel when she was thirteen, and hasn't stopped since. She lives with her ball python, Fester, and two cats, Ash and Rowan.

In her spare time, she crochets, makes cloth dolls, collects antiques, books, and vintage clothing, and takes digital photographs with varying degrees of success.

Her *Beth-Hill series* is set in the area in America that contains many supernatural creatures: Wild Hunt, Vampires, Dragons, Faery and more.

It is part of the Universe that her *Jacob Lane Series, Karen Montgomery Series* and vampire trilogy, *The Shadow Series* are set in.

Follow all her books on her author page:

http://www.writers-exchange.com/Jennifer-St-Clair/

If you want to read more about other books by this author, they are listed on the following pages...

A Beth-Hill Novel (Stand Alone Novels)

Are creatures of the night and all manner of extramundane beings drawn to certain locations in the natural world? In the Midwestern village of Beth-Hill located in southern Ohio, the population is made up of its fair share of common citizens...and much more than its share of supernatural residents. Take a walk on the wild side in this unusual place where imagination meets reality.

Blood of Innocents

Ten years ago, Orien, crown prince of the Seleighe, was captured by his mortal enemies, locked in a dungeon and turned into a vampire. Six years into Orien's sentence, the Healer's brother Cullen disobeyed his mistress's orders to kill him and turned him into a vampire instead, thus sealing both their fates for all eternity.

Now both Orien and Cullen are set free. But a secret only Cullen knows lies locked inside his mind, threatening to drive him mad before he can uncover the identity of a traitor--the very elf who betrayed Orien and left them both to die in darkness.

Publisher: http://www.writers-exchange.com/blood-of-innocents/

Full Moon

Werewolves change into wolves when the moon is full. But Edward's curse only allows him to be *human* when the moon is full.

Alone and despairing, Edward hides himself away from the world. He's scraped out a meager existence for himself for almost a century in the forest he's grown to love and call home. But in the depths of a terrible winter, he stumbles across clues from the life his mother left behind in Faerie. The truth may give him the answers he needs about the source of his birthright... and the curse that holds him captive.

Publisher: http://www.writers-exchange.com/full-moon/

A Beth-Hill Novel: Jacob Lane Series

Are creatures of the night and all manner of extramundane beings drawn to certain locations in the natural world? In the Midwestern village of Beth-Hill located in southern Ohio, the population is made up of its fair share of common citizens...and much more than its share of supernatural residents.

Jacob Lane is a ten-year-old girl who's spent her life unaware of her magical heritage. After being sent to Darkbrook, a school of magic, supernatural mysteries seem to spring to life all around her and her new friends.

Book 1: The Tenth Ghost

After Jacob Lane's parents mysteriously vanish, she's sent to Darkbrook, the only school of magic in the United States. While there, she and her new friends stumble upon a series of mysterious deaths in the nine ghosts that haunt the halls of Darkbrook. These ghosts were students who died at the school over the past hundred years. Will Jacob become the tenth ghost, or can she stop a witch's reign of terror?

Publisher: http://www.writers-exchange.com/the-tenth-ghost/

Book 2: The Ninth Guest

When Jacob's friend Ophelia's family decides to open up their castle for guests, amateur paranormal sleuth Jacob Lane is invited to join in on the fun. "Spend the night in a vampire's castle and live to tell the tale!" is supposed to be a fundraiser to help Ophelia's family pay the bills. Heating a castle costs quite a bit, after all. But, after the truth of an old secret is uncovered, what began as an innocent business venture soon turns deadly when vampire hunters get involved.

For years, the vampire hunters have had only one goal: To destroy all vampires. With the help of a new friend, Jacob and Ophelia must work together to save the entire VonBriggle family from extinction.

Publisher: http://www.writers-exchange.com/the-ninth-guest/

Book 3: The Eighth Room

For two hundred years, the Selkies have kept themselves separate from those who live on land. But now the Selkies need allies or they'll be crushed by their ancient enemies, the Finfolk.

Jacob and Ophelia, students at the only school of magic in the United States, uncover a mystery that dates back to Darkbrook's beginnings. While helping clean out old storage rooms for classroom expansion, they find something that might save the Selkies from extinction. With the help of the youngest member of the Wild Hunt who are no longer so wild or terrifying, they must foil the Finfolk who desire the Selkie's destruction...or die trying.

Publisher: http://www.writers-exchange.com/the-eighth-room/

Book 4: The Seventh Secret

After a picture of Niklas, the dragons' liaison to the only school of magic in the United States, shows up in too many newspapers to count, Darkbrook is forced to go on the defensive. The secret of Darkbrook's existence has been discovered. But there are more than dragonhunters in the forest, and, as Jacob Lane, supernatural sleuth and student at Darkbrook, learns how to use her newly discovered talent of healing, she helps to right an old wrong and must battle a teenaged wizard intent on proving--once and for all--that magic is real.

Publisher: http://www.writers-exchange.com/the-seventh-secret/

Book 5: The Sixth Stone

Jacob Lane, supernatural sleuth, and Danny, her werewolf friend, stumble across an alternate world where the Wild Hunt was never bound, and Darkbrook, the school of magic they attend, was abandoned a hundred years ago.

But when the Hounds of the Hunt wish to surrender, the two students are swept up in a whirlwind of heartbreak, betrayal, and the discovery of a lost treasure.

Publisher: http://www.writers-exchange.com/the-sixth-stone/

A Beth-Hill Novella: Karen Montgomery Series

Are creatures of the night and all manner of extramundane beings drawn to certain locations in the natural world? In the Midwestern village of Beth-Hill located in southern Ohio, the population is made up of its fair share of common citizens...and much more than its share of supernatural residents. Take a walk on the wild side in this unusual place where imagination meets reality.

Karen Montgomery was an ordinary woman until she stumbled into the extraordinary... A bargain with elves worth its weight in gold. A plague of sinister ladybugs. Rogue vampire hunters, including one who tries to turn over a new leaf--with disastrous consequences. A ghostly huntsmen of the Wild Hunt wishing for redemption. Karen's life will never be the same again.

Book 1: Budget Cuts

Karen Montgomery is used to taking care of the unpleasant jobs no one else wants to deal with. When a shortage of funds forces her to fire fifteen employees from the library, she isn't happy, but the nasty task has to be done and she is, after all, the boss. But Karen finds finishing her task impossible when she can't seem to track down Ivy Bedinghaus, a night clerk she's never actually met. Once she finally does confront Ivy, she's thrust into a centuries-old conflict that makes her previous troubles radically pale in comparison.

Publisher: http://www.writers-exchange.com/budget-cuts/

Book 2: The Secret of Redemption

Karen Montgomery, librarian, finds herself embroiled in another otherworldly adventure...

A member of the Wild Hunt--ghostly myths that aren't so ghostly (or myth-like) anymore--needs help in reconciling who he once was in life and who he is now.

A little girl has gone missing. And the one most likely responsible for her disappearance is the one Karen must prove innocent.

Publisher: http://www.writers-exchange.com/the-secret-of-redemption/

Book 3: Ladybug, Ladybug

An innocent attempt to rid the library of a plague of ladybugs turns sinister when a rogue vampire hunter gets the contract for pest control.

Ivy Bedinghaus, who works for Karen as a night clerk--along with all the vampires in Beth-Hill--are in danger, and their only hope for survival is with the help of Karen, a member of the Wild Hunt, and Russell Moore, a reformed vampire hunter.

Publisher: http://www.writers-exchange.com/ladybug-ladybug/

Book 4: Detour

One wrong turn sends Karen down a road that shouldn't exist, to the site of an old accident and an even older mystery. With reformed vampire hunter Russell Moore's help, Karen finds the key to the mystery. But Russ keeps his own secrets...some of which are deadly.

When old friends from Russ' past come to call, Karen realizes his secrets might just mean his doom. After a terrible incident three years ago, before Karen met him, Russ wants only to live the rest of his life quietly in Beth-Hill. But his secret might not allow him the new lease on life Russ longs for.

Publisher: http://www.writers-exchange.com/detour/

Companion Story: Russ' Story: Capture

Long before Russell Moore ever met supernatural sleuth Karen Montgomery or set foot in Beth-Hill, he was a vampire hunter, possibly the best vampire hunter of all. He brought down whole nests of vampires, caring little about the consequences of his actions. Anyone who lived with or helped the vampires became enemies to be slaughtered.

So what kind of an idiot would capture a ruthless vampire hunter without a conscience and try to reform him?

Ethan Walker was that idiot. Wanting to protect his family, Ethan set out to prove to Russ that vampires weren't all evil, soulless creatures. If Russ would allow himself to witness their lives, see their humanity, surely he and other vampire hunters like him would let them live in peace. *Surely?*

Publisher: http://www.writers-exchange.com/capture/

A Beth-Hill Novel: The Abby Duncan Series

Are creatures of the night and all manner of extramundane beings drawn to certain locations in the natural world? In the Midwestern village of Beth-Hill located in southern Ohio, the population is made up of its fair share of common citizens...and much more than its share of supernatural residents. Take a walk on the wild side in this unusual place where imagination meets reality.

Situated in Beth-Hill, where imagination meets reality, is The Rose Emporium, owned by elderly and not-a-little-odd Rose Duncan. The large Victorian house smackdab in the middle of nowhere is a cross between a pawn shop and an antique store that caters to supernatural creatures needing to barter. Rose's twenty-something niece, Abby Duncan, discovers that the world isn't made up of just run-of-the-mill, ordinary humans but an entire spectrum of unusual beings. With her preconceptions about what's normal and what's not turned upside-down, Abby is in for a whole lot of startling truths, mysteries-- about herself and the people and places around her--and danger.

Novella 1: By Any Other Name

Woodturner Abby Duncan decides to sell her spindles at a local Renaissance Festival with only some success. After all, no one really spins their own yarn anymore, do they? While there, she discovers that one of her newfound friends is not what he appears--and his secret is about to get him killed!

Publisher: http://www.writers-exchange.com/by-any-other-name/

Book 2: The Uncrowned Queen

Abby Duncan's elderly Aunt Rose has always been a bit odd. And now she's off on a mysterious trip, leaving Abby behind to run the Rose Emporium, an unusual sort of antique shop. Such an extraordinary store would have been a perfect place for Seth and the others, her friends from the Renaissance Festival, to take a break from traveling between Faires. But when tragedy strikes and Abby and the others discover the true nature of the Rose Emporium, they'll have to travel into Faerie itself before their tightknit group is whole again.

Abby doesn't know much about her family history, but she's about to find out the truth...whether she likes it or not.

Publisher: http://www.writers-exchange.com/the-uncrowned-queen/

Book 3: Coming Soon!

Secrets When in Shadow Lie

Twelve years ago, Ryan Grey was cursed by a witch to hide a secret. He's lived with the curse of being unable to die permanently, and, over the years he's slowly losing the memory of his past until almost nothing remains.

But now, after a chance meeting with an elf named Zipporah, he discovers the key to unlocking the secret and breaking the curse once and for all...if he can survive the breaking.

Publisher: http://www.writers-exchange.com/secrets-when-in-shadow-lie/

The Dead Who Do Not Sleep

Will Spark only wants a good night's sleep after a night of drinking. Instead, two thugs bang on his door, demanding answers to questions he can't understand. And then they killed him...

Publisher: http://www.writers-exchange.com/the-dead-who-do-not-sleep/

A Beth-Hill Novel: The Shadows Trilogy

Are creatures of the night and all manner of extramundane beings drawn to certain locations in the natural world? In the Midwestern village of Beth-Hill located in southern Ohio, the population is made up of its fair share of common citizens...and much more than its share of supernatural residents. Take a walk on the wild side in this unusual place where imagination meets reality.

A Dreamer dreams the future when the past is not yet laid to rest. Ten years ago, a plague swept across the Seven Kingdoms. Ten years ago, the Queen of Iomar's son was exiled and named the author of the magical plague. Now, in the present, Terrin works to complete his ultimate goal: Control of the Seven Kingdoms using his son's power to supplement his own. But his attempt at dominion meets resistance and the fate of the world rests in the unlikely hands of an exiled prince, a Dreamer, and a vampire...

Book 1: The Prince of Shadows

When Alban's father Terrin appeared at the castle door with a vampire in tow and apologies on his lips, Alban fell under his spell just like everyone else and welcomed him home. But Terrin didn't return to live quietly in his brother's kingdom. He had other plans and, with Alban's untrained powers at his disposal, he begins his ruthless plan to destroy the Seven Kingdoms and rule them all, beginning with his brother's death.

Terrin engineers events to cast the blame on his nephew, Teluride, intending to see the boy executed for his father's murder. But there are those who would thwart Terrin in his mad plan for power, and Alban forms an unlikely alliance with Skade, the reclusive Queen of Iomar, and Terrin's slave, a young vampire with no memory of his name or origins. Although the future looks grim, Alban and the vampire attempt to stop Terrin...and they almost succeed.

A darker history lies at the heart of Terrin's treachery, and only Skade knows the true reason why Terrin would murder his own brother and attempt to destroy both Alban and the vampire to achieve his goals. The Ghost who resides in Skade's mirror--her servant and thrall--holds one of the keys to Terrin's madness. Unfortunately, more than one person wishes for the past to remain the past and the future to hold no shadows of what might have been...

Publisher: http://www.writers-exchange.com/the-prince-of-shadows/

Book 2: Lost In Shadows

Events set in motion ten years ago come to a head as Skade, the reclusive Queen of Iomar, and Nicodemus, who is imprisoned by Skade, struggle to free Alban and the vampire from Terrin's grasp. Old secrets come to light when Skade's exiled son is forced to face his past--or die trying to redeem himself once and for all. Can the crimes of the past truly be forgiven? Only time will tell...and time is running out.

Publisher: http://www.writers-exchange.com/lost-in-shadows/

Book 3: Bound In Shadows

With his power crushed, brother to the king and father to Alban, Terrin is forced to take drastic measures to regain his sons after they are freed and harness the power they possess. But he has an ally inside the healer's house where they are recovering who works to further his plans. The Queen of Iomar, Skade's son, courts redemption to try to save his mother's life, and the vampire who no longer remembers his own name dreams a dream that might save them all...or damn them if success is thwarted.

Publisher: http://www.writers-exchange.com/bound-in-shadows/

A Beth-Hill Novel: Wild Hunt Series

Are creatures of the night and all manner of extramundane beings drawn to certain locations in the natural world? In the Midwestern village of Beth-Hill located in southern Ohio, the population is made up of its fair share of common citizens...and much more than its share of supernatural residents. Take a walk on the wild side in this unusual place where imagination meets reality.

The Wild Hunt roamed the forest outside of Beth-Hill until the Council bound them for a hundred years. Nevertheless, a century of existence has made an indelible mark not easily forgotten for these ghostly myths that are no longer so ghostly or myth-like...

Book 1: Heart's Desire

The Wild Hunt roamed the forest outside of Beth-Hill until the Council bound them for a hundred years--a lifetime for a human but only a passing thought to one such as Gabriel, Master of the Wild Hunt. As the Council's binding draws to a close, old enemies reappear to ensure that the Wild Hunt is bound once more--to a creature much worse than the Council has been.

Publisher: http://www.writers-exchange.com/hearts-desire/

Book 2: Fire and Water

As a young vampire, Erialas Morgan brought his mother back to life with a spell that shouldn't exist, shouldn't have worked...perhaps shouldn't have been performed at all. Desperation and love are his only excuses for doing the unthinkable.

There are others who wish to use that same spell for their own gain--and to destroy the Wild Hunt once and for all. Caught in the middle of a war between the Morgan clan of vampires and their human kin, Erialas turns to the Hunt for help. But even Gabriel, the Master of the Wild Hunt, may not be able to stop the tide of death and destruction once it turns.

Publisher: http://www.writers-exchange.com/fire-and-water/

Book 3: The Lost

Almost sixty years ago, Darkbrook, the only school of magic in the United States, opened its doors to students of decidedly different natures, sending out letters of invitation to the elves, the dragons, and the vampires. The three who responded to the invitation banded together despite their differences but vanished only weeks later along with an entire classroom full of students and their teacher after a field trip gone horribly wrong.

The Wild Hunt has healed and the Hounds have grown closer together, keeping Darkbrook's forest safe and secure for those who live there. Malachi, one of the eldest members of the Wild Hunt, has adapted to Josiah's spell to help him see, but when a demon boy trapped in the body of a human body for sixty years inside the school disrupts the newfound calm, the Hunt--and those they protect--are thrust into a struggle that should have ended long ago when a vampire, an elf, and a dragon vanished into the Mists.

Publisher: http://www.writers-exchange.com/the-lost/

Book 4: A Glint of Silver

Jericho is a vampire who wants is to live away from the Richmond household of vampires led by his ruthless father Connor. When Jericho tries to escape, Connor punishes him and leaves him to die. Tristan is determined to be the one to bring Jericho back, but he can't see him suffer for wanting a normal life. As long as Connor lives, Jericho will never be safe or free. As long as Connor *lives*...

Publisher: http://www.writers-exchange.com/a-glint-of-silver/

Book 5: All That Glitters

As a member of the cruel Morgan Household of vampires, twelve-year-old Arthur Morgan has been abused all his life.

Maya, a water fairy, shows him just how horrible and twisted the household he's grown up is. With her help, and the unexpected help of an adult vampire, Arthur attempts to escape.

Can he become something more than what his father has decreed?

The Chelsea Chronicles

Normally a quiet, serene place, Chelsea Kingdom seems like the perfect location for a centuries' old vampire to blend in and live a normal life, even escape hunters and an angry mob. Unfortunately, his timing couldn't be worse...

Book 1: So You Want to be a Vampire

Chelsea Kingdom is usually a pretty quiet place but recent murders--committed by a vampire--upset the calm. Newcomer to town, Vlad Dhalgren wants only to blend in and live a normal life. He quickly learns that isn't possible, given that other vampires have been hiding in the shadows around the castle--in plain sight--for years.

Despite her lineage, Anna Everett, the crown princess of the Kingdom of Chelsea, isn't a wizard like her father, which means she will never be Queen. She has only one friend, Valerian Moreton--Val--who has secrets he's never shared that could get him *and* Anna killed...

Publisher: http://www.writers-exchange.com/so-you-want-to-be-a-vampire/

Book 2: Transformation

As Anna, crown princess of Chelsea, adjusts to life as a vampire after recent events, Vlad plans for a future he has no real hope to seeing come to pass due to injuries sustained while attempting to save Anna's life. But, as life goes on for Anna and her friend Valerian "Val" Moreton, it changes for others--some of whom are not quite what they seem...

Publisher: http://www.writers-exchange.com/transformation/

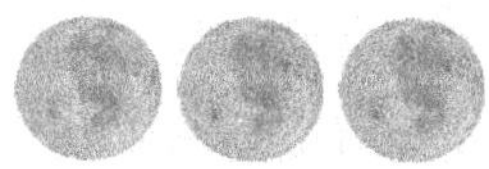

You can find ALL our books up on our website at:

http://www.writers-exchange.com

All Jennifer's books:

http://www.writers-exchange.com/Jennifer-St-Clair/

all our fantasy novels:

http://www.writers-exchange.com/category/genres/fantasy/

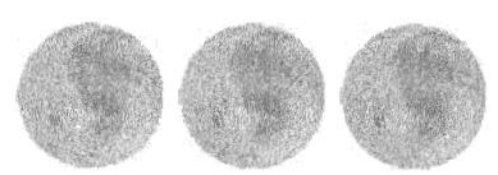